Logan McLaughlin was perfection under her hands.

Trinity wanted more. And took it.

Tilting her head, she deepened the kiss and he countered instantly, swirling his tongue forward to find hers, heightening the roar of hunger pounding through her veins. His mouth. God, the things it was doing to her. The things it could do.

And then all at once, his lips disappeared and she swayed forward, desperate to get them back on hers. Instead, he leaned in and nuzzled her ear.

"How'd I do?" he murmured. "Close enough to what you were going for?"

Trinity laughed, because what else could she do? "Yeah. That was perfect."

He'd been on to her scheme the entire time. Of course. What had she thought, that a man with commitment and white picket fences written all over him might actually go for a woman like her, who'd turned her independence into a shield? That he'd been as into the kiss as she had, almost forgetting it wasn't real?

Never in a million years would they make sense together—unless it was fake.

This was a great place for goodbye. But for some reason, Trinity was having a very difficult time taking her hands off her partner.

* * *

From Enemies to Expecting
is part of Mills & Boon Desire's
Love and Lipstick series—For four female executives,
mixing business with pleasure leads to love!

FROM ENEMIES TO EXPECTING

BY
KAT CANTRELL

First Published in Great Britain 2017
By Mills & Boon, an imprint of HarperCollins*Publishers*
1 London Bridge Street, London, SE1 9GF

ISBN: 978-0-263-06842-9

Our policy is to use papers that are natural, renewable and recyclable
products and made from wood grown in sustainable forests. The logging
and manufacturing processes conform to the legal environmental
regulations of the country of origin.

Printed and bound in Great Britain
by CPI Antony Rowe, Chippenham, Wiltshire

USA TODAY bestselling author **Kat Cantrell** read her first Mills & Boon novel in third grade and has been scribbling in notebooks since she learned to spell. She's a Harlequin So You Think You Can Write winner and a Romance Writers of America Golden Heart® Award finalist. Kat, her husband and their two boys live in north Texas.

One

Logan McLaughlin hated losing. So of course the fates had gifted him with the worst team in the history of major league baseball. Losing had become an art form, one the Dallas Mustangs seemed determined to master. Short of cleaning house and starting over with a new roster, Logan had run out of ideas to help his ball club out of their slump.

Being the team's owner and general manager should be right up his alley. Logan's dad had run a billion-dollar company with ease and finesse for thirty years. Surely Logan had inherited a little of Duncan McLaughlin's business prowess along with a love of baseball and his dad's dot-com fortune?

Ticket sales for the Mustangs' home games said otherwise. A losing streak a mile long was the only reason Logan had agreed to the ridiculous idea his publicist had put forth, otherwise, he'd never have darkened the door of a reality game show. As last-ditch efforts went, this one took the cake.

But, as his publicist informed him, Logan had run out of charity golf tournaments, and they hadn't helped drive ticket sales anyway. Short of winning games—which he was working on, via some intricate and slow trade agreements—he needed to get public support for his team another way. Now.

Exec-ution's set teemed with people. Logan stood in the corner nursing a cup of very bad coffee because it was that or rip off someone's head due to caffeine withdrawal. He should have stopped at Starbucks on the way to the studio, but who would have thought that an outfit that asked its contestants to be on the set at 5:00 a.m. wouldn't have decent coffee? He was stuck in hell with crap in a cup.

"Logan McLaughlin." A pretty staffer with an iPad in the crook of her elbow let her gaze flit over the other contestants until she zeroed in on him standing well out of the fray. "Care to take a seat? We're about to begin filming."

"No, thanks. I'll stand," he declined smoothly with a ready smile to counter his refusal.

Chairs were for small people; at six-four, 220, Logan hadn't fit in most chairs since eleventh grade. Plus, he liked being able to see the big picture at a glance.

A soft-looking middle-aged man in a suit nodded at Logan. "Thought I recognized you. I'm a Yankees fan from way back. Used to watch you pitch, what, ten years ago?"

"Something like that," Logan agreed easily.

The Yankees had let him go eight years ago, but who was counting when the career he'd poured his heart and soul into ended in a failed Tommy John surgery? His elbow still ached occasionally, just in case he didn't have enough reminders that his days on the mound were over.

"Man, you were great. Sorry about the arm." The man shook his head. "Shame you can't get any of your starters shaped up. The Mustangs could use a guy with your skill."

Yeah. Shame. Logan nodded his thanks. He tossed his crap in a cup into a trash can and crossed his arms over the void in his chest that owning a baseball team hadn't filled. It was getting harder and harder to convince himself that his glory days were not behind him.

Winning games. Ticket sales. Merchandise sales. These were things that would fix that void. And when he won *Exec-ution*, sports news outlets would have something to do with his name besides dragging it through the mud.

The staffer called a few more people to take seats around the boardroom table. A photograph of the downtown Dallas skyline peeked through the faux window behind the table. Crew members buzzed around the cameras, and a few tech guys sat behind glass in a control room, wearing headsets. The host of the show sat at the head of the table, hands carefully laced in front him, with perfectly coiffed hair and a bogus TV smile.

"Let's have a good show!" The staffer melted away, and Well-Coiffed Guy launched into his spiel.

"Hi, everyone! I'm Rob Moore, your host for *Exec-ution*, where executives compete in two-person teams in an entrepreneurial challenge designed to showcase the ability to run a business. The winners get one hundred thousand dollars for charity. Losers? Executed!"

Logan rolled his eyes as the host smacked the table with his trademark chopping motion. So cheesy.

A commotion caught everyone's attention. A dark-haired woman strode onto the set with the pretty staffer dogging her heels.

Logan promptly forgot about the smarmy host and fake boardroom in favor of watching the real show—the dark-haired woman walking.

She moved liked an outfielder with a batter's home run in the works: fast, purposeful and determined not to let that ball go over the wall. Maybe she could teach his guys a few things about how to hustle.

The closer she got, the more interesting she became. A wide stripe of pink ran down the left side of her hair. The right side had been shorn close to her head in an asymmetrical cut that made Logan feel off-kilter all at once. Or maybe that was due to her thick, black Cleopatra-style eye makeup, which was far sexier than it should be.

She had everyone's attention exactly where she wanted it—on her. A woman dressed in a slim-fit, shocking pink suit cut low enough to allow her very nice breasts to peek out clearly expected people to notice her.

"Sorry I'm late," she offered the host. Her throaty voice thrummed through Logan in a way he hadn't been *thrummed* in a very long time. Not since his pitching days, when baseball groupies had been thick on the ground, which he'd taken advantage of far less than he could have.

This lady in pink had the full package, and then some. For some other guy.

Logan avoided packaged women like the plague, as they often came with nasty surprises once you unwrapped them. He liked his women simple, unaffected and open, a younger version of the best woman he knew—his mom.

Didn't mean he couldn't appreciate a gorgeous woman with a sexy voice.

Pink Lady drew even with Logan, electing to stand despite open seats at the table and ice-pick heels on her feet that couldn't be comfortable.

"I tried to explain that we'd already started filming," the staffer told Rob Moore in a hushed voice that carried across the whole set. "She barged in anyway."

"It's okay," the host said with a crafty smile. He waltzed over to them, his gaze cutting back and forth between Logan and the lady in pink at his side. "Oh, I like this. Very nice. Bad girl meets all-American boy. The viewers will love it."

"Love what?" Logan glanced down at his blue Mustangs T-shirt and jeans and then at the dark-haired woman. Moore's comment sank in. "You want us to be teammates? I don't think so."

That was not happening. But Moore had already moved on to the next couple, both of whom looked relieved with their matches.

The sinking feeling in Logan's stomach bottomed out. Pink Lady had crossed her arms under her spectacular breasts, shoving them upward so that they strained against the fabric of her suit. He averted his eyes as she started tapping out a staccato rhythm with one stiletto.

"What's wrong with being my teammate?" Her agitation pushed her voice up a notch. "You don't think I have any business savvy because of the tongue piercing. That's crap and you know it."

A...*tongue* piercing? Instantly, he envisioned exactly what skills a woman with a steel bar through her tongue might have. And they all centered on being naked. With her mouth on his flesh as she pleasured him.

Dragging his thoughts out of the gutter took entirely too much will. That's why he liked unassuming, unsexy, *uneverything* women.

"I didn't even notice that," he informed her truthfully and tried to stop himself from catching a glimpse of the piercing. "My objections have nothing to do with you."

That part was patently false. It had everything to do with the fact that she had *distraction* written all over her. He'd have to get a new teammate, no question.

For God knew what reason, she laughed, and that did a hell of lot more than *thrum* in Logan's gut.

"I have a BS meter with new batteries," she said. "Look around, honey. Everyone else has been paired. Can we get with the program?"

Logan peered down at his new teammate's fingernail, which had landed in the dead center of his chest. Then he glanced back up at her incredibly disturbing eyes. They were a shade of ice blue that seemed so much more stark and unique than they should, probably because of her eye makeup.

"I'm with the program." He reeled back the curl of awareness that her finger had aroused. "The question is, are you? I wasn't late."

"Five a.m. is an ungodly hour, and I was only fifteen minutes late. You can't hold that against me."

Yeah, actually he could. *He'd* been on time and so had everyone else. But since it did appear as if all the other teams had been set, he sighed. "Fine. You're forgiven. What did you say your industry is again?"

"I didn't. What did you say your name is again?"

The point wasn't lost on him. He'd completely abandoned civility with this pink curveball, and his mama had taught him better than that. He stuck out a hand. "Logan McLaughlin. Owner and general manager of the Dallas Mustangs."

"Sports is your thing, I see. The lack of dress-up clothes threw me." She glanced at his Mustangs shirt, and then slipped her hand in his for what should have been a perfunctory shake.

The moment her palm slid against his, a shock zinged up his arm, arrowing straight for his groin. He let it ride because it was that powerful and, God, he hadn't felt anything like it in ages. Her eyelids drifted downward a touch, and she peeked up at him from under her lashes, clearly affected by it as well.

"I own suits," he muttered, loath to release her and completely aware that he should have ended the hand-shake at least thirty seconds ago. "I'd rather go naked than wear one."

What was he *doing*?

Get a grip, McLaughlin. This woman was the polar opposite of his type, and flirting with her could only lead to disaster, especially since they were supposed to be focused on winning. Unfortunately, he had a feeling the disaster train had already pulled out of the station.

"Naked is my favorite, too." Her voice had dropped back into the throatiness he much preferred. That was not going to work, either. "Trinity Forrester. Yes, as in the holy trinity, the chick in *The Matrix* and the river. I've heard all the jokes, so save them."

"I guess I'm not allowed to ask if you're overly re-ligious, then."

She smiled, leaning in close enough to share a whiff of her exotic scent that of course only added to her al-lure.

"If you do, you get my standard answer. 'Any man

in a ten-foot radius is expected to treat me like a god-
dess. You can get started worshipping me any time.'"

Oh, she'd like that, wouldn't she? His eyes narrowed.

If they were going to be teammates, they had to get a
few things straight. No flirting. No throaty voices coupled with come-hither glances. Logan called the shots,
and Ms. I've Heard All the Jokes had better be able to
keep up. Sexy heels were optional.

The cameras had captured every word of the exchange. So far, so good.

The more the cameras tuned in to Trinity, the more
times the producers would overlay her name and Fyra
Cosmetics on the screen. You couldn't buy better advertising than that, and Fyra needed all the positive
press it could get.

Trinity Forrester would get that press come hell or
high water. Nothing could be allowed to happen to her
company, the one she and her three best friends from
college had built from a concept and a dream. Thanks
to an internal saboteur, Fyra was struggling. As the
chief marketing officer, Trinity took the negative publicity personally. It was her job to stop the hemorrhag-
ing. *Exec-ution* was step one in that plan.

Otherwise, she'd be in her office hard at work on the
campaign for Formula-47, the new product they'd hoped
to launch in the next couple of weeks.

Mr. McLaughlin still had her hand in his as if he
might not let go. Perfect. The more enthralled he was,
the easier it would be to take charge. Men never paid
attention to her unless they wanted to get her into the
sack, mostly because that was the way she preferred it.
Sex was the only thing she'd ever found worth doing
with a man.

She smiled at Logan for good measure. He had good ole Texas boy baked into his DNA. Toss in his longish brown hair that constantly fell in his face and his casual clothes, and yeah, Logan McLaughlin was the epitome of the all-American type. Also known as a nice guy.

Nice guys were always hiding something not so nice, and she'd learned her lesson a long time ago when it came to trusting men—don't. A surprise pregnancy in her early twenties had cured her of happily-ever-after dreams when the father of her baby took off, and then a miscarriage convinced her she wasn't mother material anyway.

"Mr. McLaughlin," she murmured. "Perhaps you'd give me my hand back so we can get to work?"

He dropped it like he'd discovered a live copperhead in his grip and cleared his throat. "Yeah. Good idea."

They retrieved a sealed envelope from the show's host, and Logan followed Trinity to an area with an easel and large pad of paper for brainstorming. Her fingers itched to mark up those pristine white pages with diagrams. If that didn't jump-start her missing muse, nothing would. Though she'd tried a lot of things.

The cameraman wedged into the small area with them, still rolling. Perfect. She'd have to come up with more outrageous things to do, just to ensure the editors had plenty to work with. Coming in late had been a stroke of brilliance. And McLaughlin's face when she'd informed him he couldn't hold fifteen minutes against her...priceless. He was obviously a rule follower. Shame.

He tore open the envelope and pulled out the contents, scanning it quickly. "We have to run a lemonade stand in Klyde Warren Park. Whichever team makes the most money wins the task and avoids execution."

"Excellent." Rubbing her hands together, she then quickly sketched out her vision for the stand, filling in small details like cross-hatching to indicate shadowing. "Orange will be the best color to paint the booth. Good contrast against green, assuming we'll be in the grassy part of the park."

Her partner loomed at her shoulder, breathing down her neck as he stretched one muscular arm out to stab the pad. "What is this?"

"A sign. That says Trinity's Lemonade."

What did the man bathe in that smelled so…manly? The clean, citrusy notes spread through her senses and caught the attention of her erogenous zones, none of which had gotten the memo that she did not go for Texas boys who looked like they lived outdoors.

The man owned a sports team, for God's sake. He'd probably need a dictionary to hold a conversation over drinks, which would no doubt include beer and a hundred TVs with a different game on each one. She and Logan were ill matched for a reality game show, let alone outside one, his rock-hard pecs aside. Her fingertip still tingled from when she'd poked him, not at all prepared for the body she'd discovered under that blue T-shirt.

"Why would we call it Trinity's Lemonade, exactly?" he asked, his deep voice rumbling in her ear. "Logan's Lemonade sounds better. Starts with the same letter."

"It's alliterative, you mean," she supplied sweetly. "I understand the dynamics of appealing to the public better than you do, honey. So let's stick with our strengths, shall we?"

She stroked a few more lines across her work of art and then yelped as her partner spun her around to face him. His mouth firmed into a flat line and he towered

over her even in her five-inch Stuart Weitzman sandals. Trinity was used to looking men in the eye, and
the fact that she couldn't do that with Logan McLaughlin put her on edge.

"You've done a really good job of not mentioning
your strengths, *darling*," he threw in sarcastically. "I
run a multimillion-dollar sports franchise. What do
you do, Ms. Forrester?"

"Haven't I mentioned it?" she tossed off casually
when she knew good and well she hadn't—on purpose.
The moment a man like him heard the word *cosmetics*,
he'd make more snap judgments and she'd had enough
of that.

At this point, though, she needed to impress upon
him that she was in her sweet spot. "I'm the CMO at
Fyra."

Blandly, he surveyed her. "The makeup company?"

"The very same. So now we're all caught up," she informed him brightly. "Marketing is my gig. Yours is figuring out which guy can hit the ball hardest. When we
have a task that requires balls, I'll let you be in charge."

This lemonade stand graphic was the first inspired
thing she'd done in weeks, which was frankly depressing. Her muse had deserted her, which was alarming
enough in and of itself, but the timing was horrific.
Fyra planned to launch its premier product in the next
ninety days. Fortunately, no one knew she'd run dry in
the creativity department. It wasn't like she could tell
her business partners that she had a mental block when
it came to Formula-47. They were counting on her.

His mouth tipped up in a slow smile that didn't fool
her for a second. "In case you've forgotten, we're partners. That means all tasks require balls, specifically
mine. Shove over and let's do this together."

Nice. Not only had he called her on her double entendre, he'd done it with a style she grudgingly appreciated. Which was the only reason she stepped a half inch
to the right, graciously offering him room at the pad.

His arm jostled hers as he took way more space than
she'd intended. The man was a solid wall of muscle,
with wide shoulders and lean hips, and yeah, of course
she'd noticed how well his jeans hugged the curve of
his rear. That part of Logan McLaughlin was a gift to
women everywhere, and she'd gotten in her share of
ogling.

Without a word, he picked up his own marker and
crossed out "Trinity's Lemonade," then scrawled,
"McLemonade" across the sign. Oh, God. That was
perfect. How dare he be the one to come up with it?

Scowling, she crossed her arms and in the process made sure to throw an elbow into his ribs. Which
promptly glanced off as if she'd hit a brick wall. And
now her elbow hurt.

"Fine," she ground out. "We'll go with yours. But
the booth will be orange."

He shrugged, shouldering her deliberately. "I didn't
have an issue with that."

The man was intolerable. Nowhere near the nice guy
she'd pegged him as, and once he opened his mouth,
totally unattractive. Or at least that was what she was
telling herself.

"Oh, yeah? So the stuff you do have issues with—
that's all getting the McLaughlin veto?" Standing her
ground shouldn't be this hard, but heels coupled with the
immovable mountain snugged next to her body threw
her off, and not solely because it was impossible to
think through the shooting pangs of awareness that she
couldn't seem to get under control.

Instead of glaring, his expression smoothed out and he took a deep breath.

"Let's start over." He extended his hand.

Because he'd piqued her curiosity, she took it and he swallowed her palm with his. Little frissons of awareness seeped into her skin at the contact.

"I'm Logan McLaughlin. I run a baseball team and our ticket sales suck. My publicist insisted that this game show would be a good way to get some eyes on the team, so here I am. Any help I can get toward that goal is appreciated."

His clear hazel eyes held hers, and his sincerity bled through her, tripping her pulse unexpectedly. Well, jeez. Honesty. What would the man think of next?

"Hi," she said because that seemed to be all her throat could summon as they stared at each other, intensity burning through her. "I'm, um, Trinity Forrester. I sell cosmetics alongside three women I love dearly. Our company stepped in a negative publicity hole, so *my* publicist came up with the brilliant idea to stick me on a TV show. I'm…not so sure that was a good move."

That made Logan laugh, and the rich sound of it wound through her with warmth that was so nice, her knees weakened. Weakness under any circumstances was not acceptable. But hardening herself against him took way more effort than it should have.

Was it so wrong to let a man like him affect her? Sure he was insufferable, pigheaded and way too virtuous for her tastes, but he had a gorgeous body, a nice smile and longish hair made for a woman's fingers. He couldn't be all bad.

"Oddly enough, I was thinking the same thing," he admitted, his eyes crinkling at the corners. "But I've changed my mind. I think we can help each other if we work together. Willing to give it a shot?"

Guess that was her answer about what else he had up his sleeve—he was going to be pleasant instead of an obstinate jackass. Strictly to mess with her head, most likely.

But she needed to work with him to benefit both of their goals. She bit her tongue and slipped her hand from his. "I can give that a shot."

They put their heads together, and true to his word, Logan listened to her ideas. She considered it a plus when he laughed at her jokes. No one had to know she secretly reveled in it.

By the end of the afternoon, they'd amassed a solid four hundred dollars and change with their McLemonade booth. God knew how. They'd fought over everything: how much to charge, where to set up, how much lemonade to put in the cups. Apparently, Mr. Nice Guy only made an appearance when he wanted something, then vanished once he got into the thick of things.

Finally, the show's producer asked them to pack up and head to the studio so they could wrap up the day's shooting. They drove separate cars to the set and met up again in the fake boardroom.

This time, Trinity grabbed a seat. An entire day on her feet, most of it on grass while wearing stilettos, was not doing her body any favors.

"Welcome back, everyone!" Rob Moore called, and the teams gathered around the table.

Logan stood at the back and Trinity pretended like she didn't notice the vacant seat by her side. All the other teammates sat next to each other. Fine by her. She and her partner got on like oil and water and had only figured out how to work together because they'd had to.

"We've tallied all the sales, and I must say, this was an impressive group of teams." The host beamed at them. "But the winners are Mitch Shaughnessy and John Roberts!"

Disappointed, Trinity clapped politely as the winning team high-fived each other and jogged to the head of the table to claim the giant check made out to St. Jude Children's Hospital. That was the important thing—the money was going to a good cause.

"The winning team's proceeds were..." Rob Moore paused for dramatic effect. "Four hundred and twenty-eight dollars. Impressive!"

Oh, dear God. They'd lost by a measly twenty-five dollars? She thought about banging her head on the table, but that wouldn't put the cameras on her face with a nice graphic overlay stating her company's name. But what if there was a way to get some additional airtime? The cameras were still rolling, panning the losers as the host launched into his trademark parting comments.

"Fire up the electric chair, boys," he cried. "We've got some executions to perform!"

This was the cheesiest part of the show, which she'd hoped to avoid. She had a good idea how to do that and get some cameras on her at the same time.

Pushing her chair backward with a sharp crack, she bolted to her feet and charged over to her partner, poking her finger in his chest with a bit more force than she'd intended. But she'd gotten the cameraman's attention, and that was all that mattered.

"This is all your fault, McLaughlin. We would have won if it wasn't for you."

His gaze narrowed, and he reached up to forcibly re-move her finger from his person. "What are you talking about? This ship started sinking the second we were paired. Bad girl meets all-American boy. *Please.* What they should have called us was train meets wreck."

That struck her as such a perfect way to describe the day that she almost laughed, but she bit it back. She could admire his wit later, over a glass of wine as she celebrated the fact that she never had to see him again. "You know what your problem is?"

"I've got no doubt you're about to tell me," he offered and crossed his arms in the pose that she'd tried—and failed—to ignore all day. When he did that, his biceps bunched up under his shirt sleeves, screaming to be touched. She just wanted to feel one once. Was that so much to ask?

"Someone needs to. Otherwise, you'd walk around with that rule book shoved up your...butt," she amended, lest the producers cut the whole exchange due to her potty mouth. "Some rules are made to be broken. That's why we lost. Apply for sainthood on your own time."

His expression heated and not in a good way. "Are you saying I'm a Goody Two-shoes?"

"If the shoe fits, wear it," she suggested sweetly. "And that's not even the worst of your problems."

He rolled his eyes, fire shooting from his gaze, and she almost caved, because he was really pissed and while she wanted the cameras on them, she also felt like crap for poking at him. But when he got hot and bothered, he lost all his filters and focused on noth-ing but her.

That, she liked.

"Oh, I've gotta hear this. Please, enlighten me."

"You're attracted to me and you can't stand it." That

was like the pot calling the kettle black, though she scarcely wanted to admit that to herself, let alone out loud.

"I'm sorry, what?"

"You heard me."

Her finger ended up back on his chest. Oops. It was hard and delicious and there was something super hot about how immovable he was. Logan was solid, the kind of guy who might actually stick around when unexpected challenges cropped up. Sometimes a girl needed a strong shoulder. He had two.

"I heard you," he growled and went to smack away her finger—she'd assumed—but he crushed her palm to his chest, holding it captive with his hand. "What I meant was, that's the craziest thing you've said so far today."

The cameraman had zoomed in on their discussion. She noted the lens from the corner of her eye and nearly smiled.

You couldn't buy this kind of exposure. This time tomorrow—with her help—this clip would go viral: *Two executives melt down on the set of a reality TV show.* Viewers would see a strong woman not taking any crap from her male partner. As long as they spelled Fyra correctly, it should amp up the positive publicity and counter the negative.

"Get ready for more crazy, because not only are you attracted to me, you can't stop thinking about what it would be like to kiss me. Admit it. You're curious about the tongue piercing."

"Of course I am," he bit out, fuzzing her brain at the same time.

He was? Fascinated, she zeroed in on him, and yeah, there was a whole lot more than agitation in his expression. Logan McLaughlin, official Boy Scout of major league baseball, had never kissed a woman with a tongue piercing. And he wanted to.

Heat and a thick awareness flooded all the places between them. His heart thumped under her palm, strong but erratic, which perfectly mirrored the stuff going on under her own skin.

"What red-blooded male wouldn't be curious," he murmured. "When there's only one reason to have a steel bar through your tongue—to pleasure a man."

His eyelids shuttered for a beat, and when he opened them, his eyes held so much wicked intent, her pulse bobbled. Caught in his hot gaze, she swayed toward him, her hand fisting his shirt. "One way to find—"

His mouth captured hers before she'd fully registered him moving. And then all rational thought drained from her mind as Logan kissed her. The TV set melted away, the fascinated onlookers disappeared—none of it registered as he yanked her into his embrace.

Exactly where she wanted to be.

Logan McLaughlin was perfection under her hands, because *yes*, he was that hard all over. His back alone qualified as a work of art, defined with peaks and valleys that she hadn't ever felt on a man before. Imagine that. Something new to be discovered on a male body.

She wanted more. And took it.

Tilting her head, she deepened the kiss, and he countered instantly, swirling his tongue forward to find hers, taking command of the kiss, heightening the roar of hunger pounding through her veins. *His mouth.* God, the things it was doing to her. The things it could do.

And then all at once, his lips disappeared and she swayed forward, desperate to get them back on hers. Instead, he leaned in and nuzzled her ear.

"How'd I do?" he murmured. "Close enough to what you were going for?"

Trinity laughed, because what else could she do? "Yeah. That was perfect."

He'd been on to her scheme the entire time. Of course. What had she thought, that a man with commitment and white picket fences written all over him might actually go for a woman like her, who'd turned her independence into a shield? That he'd been as into the kiss as she had?

Never in a million years would they make sense together—unless it was fake.

This was a great place for goodbye. But for some reason, Trinity was having a very difficult time taking her hands off her partner.

Two

The next morning, Trinity entered the five-story glass-and-steel building that housed the cosmetics company she'd helped build with her marketing savvy and love of all things feminine. She still got a thrill out of the modern design and purple accents she and her three partners had selected, and the location just north of downtown Dallas was perfect for a single woman who owned an amazing condo in the heart of the city.

Cass had been making noises about moving the company to Austin. Trinity kept her mouth shut because Fyra's CEO had a very good reason for wanting to do so—her husband, Gage, lived there and they were expecting a baby together. Trinity didn't have anything against Austin, per se. But it was yet another example of something she had no control over. She hated anything that smacked of lack of control.

Plus, what was wrong with Gage moving his company to Dallas? Both CEOs ran large companies with lots of employees. Just because Gage was the man in the equation, why did that mean he automatically won the battle?

Trinity strode toward her office to the sounds of hoots and clapping. She took a moment to grin and wave. Obviously the footage of her kiss with Logan had made the rounds. The game show itself wouldn't air until later in the week, but she'd charmed the producer out of a clip of the kiss, starting it on its viral journey by posting it to her own social media accounts and tagging everyone she knew to share it.

Trinity wasn't one for leaving things to chance.

Cass had scheduled a meeting for first thing this morning, probably to get the full scoop. Humming, Trinity grabbed coffee and dug around until she found her iPad in her shoulder bag, then strolled to the conference room where Cass stood at the head of the table.

"Hey," Trinity called and repeated her greeting to Fyra's CFO, Alex Edgewood, and then to Dr. Harper Livingston-Gates, the chief science officer, whose faces appeared in split screen on a TV mounted on the wall. Both of them were participating in the meeting virtually since they'd abandoned Dallas the moment their husbands crooked their fingers.

Trinity sank into a seat and mentally slapped herself for being unkind.

Alex was pregnant with twins and on bed rest, so it made sense that she lived in Washington, DC, with her husband, Phillip, a United States senator. Harper's husband worked in Zurich, and Trinity didn't blame her for wanting to be in the same bed with a man as hot as Dr. Dante Gates, especially since they'd just figured out they were in love after being friends for over a decade.

Maybe Trinity was a little jealous that everyone else

had such an easy time with normal female things like falling for a great guy and having his support during pregnancy. And none of them had suffered a horrendous miscarriage that had left them feeling defective. Well, so what? Trinity had other great stuff in her life, like more men than she could shake a stick at.

Except lately, great men had been pretty scarce. The pitfalls of turning thirty. Made you think more about the definition of "great," and pseudo–frat boys with Peter Pan syndrome were not it. Unfortunately, that seemed to be the type she met at her usual haunts, which was fine for the short term.

She just wished she knew why that didn't feel like enough anymore.

Cass started off with a sly smile. "You and your reality show partner got pretty chummy. Do tell."

"All for the cameras, hon," Trinity assured her. God, what was with that pang in her gut? The kiss had been fake. On both sides—never mind that she'd liked how real it felt. "We were both interested in getting additional coverage. It worked."

Alex and Harper both murmured their disappointment that the story wasn't juicier.

"I know we've turned dissecting our love lives into a regular boardroom agenda item, but let's move on," Trinity insisted smoothly. "I'm sure Cass didn't call this meeting to talk about my partner on a reality game show."

"Actually, I did," Cass corrected. "We've got a publicity issue that's at the top of everyone's mind right now. After the mess with the leak and then the FDA approval fiasco, sales went into the toilet. We've got new problems daily as articles keep popping up in what feels to me like a smear campaign."

Felt that way to Trinity, too. Which was why it pissed her off so much. This was her territory. Her company. And someone was after it.

"Yeah, I'm aware. That's why I did the show, remember?"

"I'm not sure it's enough." Cass frowned. "I approved it since the publicist suggested it, but we need to move forward with launching Formula-47. When can you schedule time to present the marketing plan?"

"Next Monday?" Trinity suggested and started calculating exactly how screwed she was…since the campaign didn't exist. *Very* would be the precise amount of screwed.

It wasn't anyone's fault but hers, but then she'd never had a creative dry spell like this one, and she couldn't even commiserate with her friends. Recent personal events for all three ladies had driven a wedge between them, with Trinity on the wrong side of the married mom division.

Trinity hated it. She was happy for her friends, but sad that they'd all chosen lives so different from the ones they'd had. So different from the one she'd mapped out for herself. And she was pretty sure that was why her creativity had completely abandoned her when she needed it most.

The sketching she'd done on that pristine white pad while Logan peered over her shoulder had been a welcome flood of ingenuity. Maybe the medium was the key—she'd run out at lunch and pick up one of those easels. It could work.

She could totally get her muse to make an appearance, work straight through and have a brilliant campaign by Monday morning. Especially if the publicity from *Exec-ution* worked like it was supposed to. With that load off her mind, then she could concentrate on turning Formula-47 into a powerhouse wrinkle and scar cream that would put Fyra at the top of the industry.

Cass nodded and shifted focus to numbers, so Alex took the lead on that, while Trinity sank down in her seat to let her mind wander in hopes of jogging something passable from her subconscious. Didn't happen, but she had almost a week. No problem.

The easel and pad did not turn into a magic bullet. Neither did the marathon brainstorming session she called to generate ideas from her creative team. At four o'clock, she sent Melinda, Fyra's receptionist, to the office supply store to get a dozen more blank pads. The remains of the two Trinity had purchased at lunch lay in ripped and crumpled pieces on her office floor. She might have stabbed a couple of the papers with her Louboutin heels, but only because big jagged holes improved the package design she'd started on.

She didn't even have a product name, which meant she had no business trying to design the packaging. Her creative process required building blocks, and the name always came first, but she'd been desperate to make *some* kind of progress. Formula-47 would be Fyra's premier product and as the CMO, Trinity should and would take on the heaviest lifting. Her creative team had enough on their plates with managing the rest of Fyra's marketing juggernaut while she buried herself in this mess.

Melinda poked her head in the door. "I've got your pads. Also, Lara from Gianni Publicity Group is here. She doesn't have an appointment. Shall I send her away?"

The publicist. Great. That was exactly what Trinity needed right now—a reminder that Cass had hired an outside firm to do Trinity's job. And Lara's big contribution thus far had landed Trinity in the arms of a do-gooder Texas boy who kissed like a wicked fantasy.

Logan McLaughlin was a name she should have forgotten by now. For God knew what reason, it still rattled around in her head, heating up places that shouldn't be heating at the thought of a rugged, lean-hipped outdoorsy guy who wasn't her type.

She sighed. "No, it's okay. I'll see her."

Lara Gianni rushed into the office, long hair streaming behind her as the chic woman grabbed Trinity by the shoulders and kissed both cheeks, Italian style. "You brilliant, brilliant lady. Logan McLaughlin is *magnifico*."

"Back off. I saw him first," Trinity said drily. Was the woman reading minds now? "Why is he magnificent again? Please tell me it's because you've got good news."

The publicist laughed. "The best. Your video has already been shared over half a million times, and the response? Amazing. People love you two together. The comments are priceless. Love on the set of a TV show is brilliant marketing."

"Wait a minute. Love on a TV show? It was an entrepreneurial game show, not *The Bachelor*." The look on Lara's face gave Trinity a very bad feeling. "The public was supposed to see the name Fyra and think positive thoughts about it. That's how you sold the idea to us."

"That was before you went in a whole different direction. One I love! You're truly brilliant."

Yeah, that part was clear. What wasn't clear was what the hell Lara was talking about. "I didn't go in a different direction. We lost the game and I had to do something extra. I kissed my partner. Voilà, now Fyra is all over social media."

"No." Lara shook her head. "*You* are all over social media. They like the romance you unwittingly created. I would highly recommend continuing it."

Trinity's stomach dropped into her shoes. "Continue what? There's no romance. It was one kiss."

A hot kiss. If she'd watched the footage a couple of dozen times before she'd posted it, no one had to know.

Lara shrugged. "I suggest you figure out how to make it into more than a kiss. It doesn't have to be a real relationship so long as you get yourself photographed with Logan McLaughlin. A lot. While kissing and making goo-goo eyes at each other."

The logic of it warred with the insanity. A fake relationship strictly for publicity? She couldn't. *He* wouldn't. Yet…how was that so different than a fake kiss for the same reason? Logan had jumped on that deal like a starving dog on a steak. Maybe he'd be *really* good at pretending they were a hot-and-heavy couple.

The thought unleashed a shiver that nearly unglued her. The side benefits of such an arrangement held many interesting possibilities that she could not ignore, like enticing a nice guy into a walk on the wild side. How much fun would it be to corrupt the hell out of the all-American boy, especially on camera?

No. A long-term fake relationship was a whole lot different than one fake kiss. Her acting skills weren't that good. Except all at once, she couldn't figure out if she'd be feigning she was into him…or pretending she wasn't.

"No way. I can't do something like that."

Lara's brow furrowed as she pulled out her phone

and tapped a few times, then held it out to display a nearly all-red pie chart. "That's the click-through rate from your video to Fyra's website."

All the blood drained from Trinity's head. Seventy-five percent. *Seventy-five percent.* The click-through rate of her most successful social media campaign ever was 12 percent.

In the wake of the smear tactics someone had launched against Fyra, she couldn't afford to pass up this idea.

Looked like she'd be paying Mr. McLaughlin a visit. Tomorrow. *Hello, new boyfriend.*

Myra slapped the printed spreadsheet on Logan's desk and didn't bother to hide her smirk. "Told you that reality show would work."

Yes, it had. He didn't need his publicist to point out the double-digit increase in ticket sales. The Mustangs' entire front office had been buzzing about it since he'd walked in this morning. And he had Trinity Forrester, CMO, to thank.

Who would have thought that sizzling kiss would pay such huge dividends?

Duncan McLaughlin had never done *that* to get customers to open their wallets, but in Logan's defense, it hadn't been his idea. Yet he'd gotten on board with it pretty dang fast, at least once he'd realized the hot woman he'd been salivating over was not coming on to him. She'd simply found one last way to get the camera on them. As tactics went, he could find little to complain about.

Other than the fact that one bad-girl kiss later, he'd come to the uncomfortable realization that he could not wipe the feel of that tongue piercing from his memory.

His admin, Lisa, popped into his office, eyes wide. "Um, boss? You have a visitor. Ms. Forrester?"

Well, well. He leaned back in his chair as Myra's expression veered between intrigued and very intrigued. Logan had a feeling his own face might be doing something similar, so he schooled it before nodding to Lisa. "You can send her in. Thanks, Myra. I'll get back to you."

And then everything in the world of baseball ceased to exist as Trinity waltzed into his office, her off-kilter hair throwing him into a tailspin. God, how was that so sexy? On her, it was one more in-your-face reminder that she was a force to be reckoned with.

Today's outfit consisted of a deep purple suit with a micro skirt, black stockings that made her legs look a mile long and silver ankle breakers that he'd like better on his bedroom floor.

"Thanks for seeing me on short notice," she said.

That throaty voice. He'd underrated what it did to him when the sound slid down his spine. His blood woke up and sluiced through his veins in a rush that made him feel alive—only being on the mound had ever replicated that feeling.

Why her? Of all people? He'd *always* been on the lookout for a simple, uncomplicated woman who listened to country music and planned picnics. A nice woman to settle down with, who could have his babies and be the love of his life. That was how his dad had done it. That was how Logan wanted to do it. The fact that he'd yet to meet his fictional perfect lady was neither here nor there—she was out there somewhere.

And her name was not Trinity. He should not be attracted to her.

All at once, he remembered his manners and rose to

his feet, palm outstretched toward the love seat near the window that overlooked the ballpark, his favorite spot in the whole stadium as long as there wasn't a game in progress. Then it was the dugout until the bitter end.

Most general managers sat in an air-conditioned luxury box, but his players were slugging it out on the field, and in August, it wasn't unusual for the temperature to hit 110. The senior McLaughlin had regularly hit the trenches alongside his employees. Logan could do the same.

Instead of taking the offered seat, Trinity slid a steamy once-over all the way down his body. "You're wearing a suit. What was it you said about those?"

I'd rather go naked.

The unspoken quote hung in the air between them, dissolving into a dense awareness that answered one lingering question on his mind since that kiss—whether or not he misremembered how deeply she'd gotten under his skin with all her innuendo.

He'd recalled it perfectly.

"I'm being a grown-up today," he croaked and cleared his throat.

"Oh, yeah, I once thought about being one of those for Halloween." She shrugged with a smile that he felt in his gut. "By the way, I like you in a suit."

"What can I do for you, Ms. Forrester?"

The sooner he got her out of his office, the sooner he could get back to work. Or take a cold shower. The last thing he should do was give her an advantage, or she'd railroad him into doing her bidding before he'd fully surfaced from being whacked upside the head by all the pheromones.

"You can call me Trinity." She jerked her chin toward the desk, flinging the dark swath of hair into motion.

She hadn't colored it today, strictly to throw him off, no doubt. "Talk to me about your numbers."

He glanced at the spreadsheet Myra had thrown at him to give himself a half second. What was she fishing for? "I'm happy with the results of the viral video and hopeful that when the show airs, the upward trend will continue. How about your numbers?"

"Fantastic. So good, in fact, I'm here with a proposal."

The way she said it brought to mind closed doors, a secret rendezvous and a solid block of time to explore just how good that bar through her tongue would feel on his body. If that ever happened, she'd completely ruin him for all other women, no doubt.

His body tightened in anticipation. *Let's find out*, it begged.

"I'm listening," he said when what he should have said was *there's the door*.

"My target customers loved the video of us together. My publicist thinks we should take advantage of it and start a public relationship. Pretend that we're dating after meeting on the show."

"That's the worst idea I've ever heard. We'd kill each other before anyone believed we were a couple."

His mind ignored his instant denial and latched on to the idea, turning it over. The timing of the video coincided with the increase in ticket sales too neatly to be a fluke. What would it hurt to capitalize on the momentum?

It could hurt *a lot*. His major objection had nothing to do with the brilliance of the idea and everything to do with his illogical reaction to her every time she got within breathing distance.

And then last night, she hadn't even been in the room

when he'd let himself envision a bedtime story about finishing that kiss with her legs wrapped around his waist. Yeah, she might be the star in his current shower fantasies. It wasn't a felony. Except he'd never in a million years have guessed that today would bring her back into his orbit, especially not this way.

Her gaze glittered with calculation. "Actually, the worst idea you'd ever heard was the one where we got paired on that stupid game show. But we made that work. *Together.* It was a team effort, and we almost won. Just think what we can accomplish with a concerted effort to exploit the public's thirst for celebrity couples. I'm offering you my complete attention to boost your ticket sales."

Her negotiation skills hit all the right notes, buttering him up, stressing the goal. Worst of all? He had an urge to say yes, simply to find out what her complete attention looked like.

Was it distasteful to use this opportunity to sate his curiosity about Trinity? A better question was how long he could do it and keep his hands off her. Not long— either he'd make good on the urge to strangle her or he'd provoke her until she kissed him again.

This idea got worse and worse the longer he thought about it.

"How do you even know I'm single?" he countered. "Maybe I've got the perfect girlfriend already and I—"

"Please don't insult me, McLaughlin." She snorted. "Or yourself. You couldn't have cut the sexual tension between us with a meat cleaver. If you do have a girlfriend and you can still kiss me like that, you're not the man I assume you are."

He scowled, and not just because of her excellent point.

"I get it now." He nodded sagely. "This is a ploy to earn yourself some more camera time. Attend a few Mustangs games where the general manager's hot girlfriend would most definitely be a subject of interest."

Boldly, she contemplated him, not at all bothered by his half-assed accusations. "What if it is? Does that automatically make it a bad idea? My reasons for liking this plan have nothing to do with the reasons you should agree. Ticket sales are the only thing that matters."

Wow. He shook his head. When you called a spade a spade with Trinity Forrester, she turned over a full house. "Let me make sure I've got this straight. You're suggesting we manufacture a relationship. Date each other, be seen at some events. And the public is going to approve of this by spending a lot of money?"

"We're going to help them do that with ad campaigns heavily laced with click bait. But, yeah. Get your publicist involved. Talk to your marketing people. Let's make it a party and get some eyes on our individual brands."

Not only did everything she was saying make sense, she had a unique way of presenting it that appealed to him. That alone ruffled his nerves. "How exactly are we going to date and manage to be civil to each other?"

Like that was the biggest issue.

"Who said we were?" Her blue eyes glowed as she caught his gaze. "Part of what sizzles about us is the way we clash. It translates really well on camera. Didn't you watch the clip?"

He might have watched the video a few times, and there wasn't a good way to pretend she was wrong. Nor could he forget how arguing with her had exploded into the heat of that kiss. "So not only are we supposed to fake date, but we're also supposed to have knock-down, drag-out fights in public, too?"

That was way over the line. Logan and his temper were old enemies, and bad decisions followed when he allowed his emotions off the leash. He'd left his hot-head days behind him when he bought the Mustangs. A team owner had to play it cool, and thus far, he'd call his newfound calm a success.

Until Trinity.

She was the only person of his acquaintance who threatened his composure on a minute-by-minute basis.

She shrugged. "Let me be clear. I'll do whatever it takes to get you to agree to this. If you want me to be nice and sweet and smile at your fans, I will."

Waltzing closer, she let her fingers trail down the front of his shirt, reminding him of the last time she'd done that—right before he'd tested out kissing a woman with a bar through her tongue.

As if she'd read his mind, her gaze instantly caught fire and swept him with a thousand licks of heat as she let her eyes wander down his body in a slow perusal that almost had him squirming. But he had far more control over his body than that—any athlete worth his salt had enormous discipline. Losing his pitching arm hadn't become an excuse to sit on the couch and get fat.

"Logan," she murmured throatily, splattering his control to hell and back as his lower half went hard. "If you want me to wear leather and carry around a whip because you like the bad-girl persona that *Execution* coated me with, I would be happy to oblige. Tell me what it will take."

Now that was an interesting proposition. His imagination took off at a brisk trot, and it was nearly impossible to rein it back in. "We'd have to make it look real."

Guess it was too late to pretend he wasn't considering it.

"Sure. Lots of public kissing. Affection. Lots of making up after a good fight. Maybe you pop the question at an event with a huge diamond ring that sparkles."

Not for a thousand percent increase in ticket sales would he do something so sacred unless he meant it. "I'm not proposing to you no matter how fake it is. That's reserved for the future Mrs. McLaughlin. She deserves to be the only one to have that experience."

Something flashed in her gaze. Longing, maybe. But it was gone before he could process it and her expression hardened. "Fair enough. You play this however you want."

"You realize we have to spend time together doing things. You're going to have to pretend to like baseball. No glazed eyes when I wax poetical about Nolan Ryan."

Actually, he might do that on occasion just for fun.

"Only if you listen with rapt attention when I mention Estée Lauder," she countered with a sly smile. "I need you. Make me an offer."

"I'll think about it."

He didn't have to. There was no way he could say no. The part he had to think about was how deep this fake relationship would ultimately go. How deep he'd be willing to admit he wanted it to go. And whether he could, in fact, hold on to both his temper and his sanity while dating Trinity Forrester.

She swept from his office on a cloud of femininity and something spicy that he suspected he'd smell in his sleep for a long time to come.

Before he could remind himself of the million and one reasons it was a dangerous, horrible idea, he texted her: I'm in.

Three

Trinity sat on Logan's text message for two days. Mostly because she had no idea what to do with a fake boyfriend. Boyfriends of any sort vexed her on the whole, but one she wasn't sleeping with broke all kinds of new ground.

What did you *do* with a man outside of bed?

Should she hit a club with him? Stand at the red rope and hope someone took pictures? That seemed too chancy, and frankly, the idea of Logan McLaughlin at a techno bar with lots of smoke and pulsing lights made her laugh. And he'd probably laugh at her if she suggested it.

While it might lead to an argument that would be delicious on camera, they'd have to actually be in public for that to generate maximum publicity. She couldn't think of anything that *would* work, though. Her lack of creativity lately was bleeding into the social arena as well, and it was bothersome. Almost as bothersome as the fact that she had a marketing presentation to give to her friends and business partners on Monday and it still didn't exist.

Formula-47 used nanotechnology to heal scars and reduce wrinkles. There were thousands of ways to market such a brilliant product. She should have two presentations by now.

That's what she had to focus on, not the two-word text message from Logan McLaughlin.

I'm in. Nothing else. No *let's meet for coffee and hash this out*. No *here are my conditions and expectations*. What? Was she supposed to do all the dirty work and organize everything? He had a stake in this, too.

By Thursday, she was ready to bite off the head of the next person who poked their toe into her office. When her phone beeped, she nearly shut it off. But then she saw Logan's name blinking at her. Eyes narrowed, she thumbed up the text message.

Charity gala tomorrow night. Guaranteed to have lots of cameras and press. Formal dress. Pick you up at 8.

Men. Logan had his share of nerve, assuming she could pull a formal ensemble together in less than thirty-six hours, not to mention she'd have to beg Franco for a last-minute appointment to get her hair done. Her regular nail girl was out of town, too. Trinity groaned and pushed back from her desk to go spend the rest of the afternoon shopping for the perfect dress to drive a man wild.

Logan McLaughlin totally deserved to spend the entire evening in the most painful state possible for springing this on her at the last minute. And if she secretly wanted to kiss him for getting her out from behind her desk and away from the reminders that her career might be circling the drain—she'd keep that to herself.

Miraculously, Franco had a cancellation, he personally found a replacement nail technician for her, and the most amazing dress fell into her lap. Logan might get a pass after all, but strictly because he'd stepped up when it counted.

When Logan knocked on the door of Trinity's penthouse loft in the Arts District, she was dressed and ready to go. Except for her lipstick. She swiped on a layer of Bohemian Rhapsody with a lip brush and dropped both into her clutch.

It was a ritual she'd always performed back when she'd dated more. Wait until he knocked and then apply lipstick, which left the guy on her doorstep for precisely the right amount of time. Enough that he'd start to wonder if maybe she wasn't dressed yet and was even at this moment throwing on clothes. Never hurt to dangle a visual in front of a man.

And then she would open the door to give him the real visual—her, dressed to the hilt in this smashing and sexy dress with cutout sides that displayed all her best features.

Except when she opened the door to Logan…in a tux…her tongue went numb and she dropped her clutch. Which he picked up for her.

Good God, did that man clean up well. The suit from the other day? Merely an appetizer to the main course of this gorgeous hunk of masculinity in a tuxedo that had clearly been custom-made for him.

Thank all that was holy that he didn't dress like that on a daily basis. The luxurious dark fabric spread across his shoulders, emphasizing the broad, dense build she shouldn't like as much as she did. Logan was too big. Too solid. Too...squeaky clean.

But the pièce de résistance was the single long-stemmed pink rose that he held out to her.

"Pink?" She took it and held it to her nose, trying not to be pleased but failing. A whole bouquet would have been overkill and completely unnecessary given that they weren't really dating.

One rose was classy. And well played.

"You wore a pink suit on the show," he said gruffly with a shrug and ran his now vacant fingers through his hair, sweeping it away from his face. "The association with that color and you is pretty much stuck in my head."

Her insides melted. She didn't know what to do with that or the best behavior vibe wafting from him. It was almost as if he'd lectured himself on the way over to remember he had a reputation for being a nice guy and maybe he should act like one.

She cleared her throat. "Thank you."

"Are you ready to go?"

Her brows rose. After three hours at the salon today, that was his comment? This sedate, boring version of Logan needed to vacate the premises, pronto, or they'd never heat it up enough for anyone to care about taking their picture.

"Don't I look ready to go?"

It would not kill him to compliment her dress. Her hair. Her punctuality. Something.

"You look like you should be spread across the floor of a Mexican restaurant," he said bluntly, with a once-over that totally contradicted his words. His gaze was more *I want to rip that dress off you* than *I want to eat tacos*.

Her hackles rose as she glanced down at her mosaic tile dress that nipped in so far at the waist it was almost two pieces. The large cutouts left her waist and hips bare, which meant when they danced, his palms would be on her bare skin. Something more along the lines of *thank you* would be highly appropriate here.

Was his vision impaired? She looked good. It wasn't arrogance. It was a fact, because she paid attention to details. If there was anything she knew how to market, it was herself.

"Well, don't hold back, honey. Tell me how you really feel about a dress that took me all day to find and set me back six grand."

"It's a little…risqué for a charity fund-raiser, don't you think?" His faint scowl told her he'd already decided the answer was yes.

"Considering Kendall Jenner wore the same dress with a different color scheme to the Met Gala, no," she countered and willed her temper back, because they hadn't even left yet. An argument now wouldn't benefit anyone, since there were no cameras around, never mind that she'd been trying to provoke him.

"I don't know who that is, but odds are good she'll never be dating me. You are. Maybe you could find a wrap?"

Hands on her bare hips, she contemplated her fake boyfriend, who was about to learn exactly how little that role entitled him to. "What's that supposed to mean? I'm not allowed to be myself because I'm dating the world's biggest Goody Two-shoes?"

His scowl grew some teeth. "Clearly we need to establish some guidelines to this…relationship. Partnership. Whatever it is. Ground rules are obviously a must."

Yeah, that was a day late and a dollar short. Honestly, she'd been a little surprised he'd agreed to this idea with no parameters.

She clapped enthusiastically. "Yay! I *love* rules."

Rules were going to go over about as well as the notion of a *wrap*. She was not putting a single thread on top of this Versace masterpiece, and he could eat his rule book. Though she was a little curious what rules he might throw down.

So she could break them all.

"Lose the sarcasm or this is going to be a very long night."

Her brows arched involuntarily. "That was always going to be true, and I'd rather lose the dress than the sarcasm."

"That can be arranged." The heat dialed up a notch as his gaze strayed to the straps around her neck that held the dress on her body.

"You wouldn't dare."

More's the pity. There was no way he'd actually strip her out of this dress simply to get his way.

Was there?

"Rule number one. Never dare me, Trinity," he said with so much wicked in his voice that she nearly pushed him on it, strictly to find out how good he was at undressing a woman in formal wear.

All at once, flashes of an ad campaign spilled into her head. A man sliding a dress off a woman and the woman stopping him before he reveals her scar. Cut to a shot of Formula-47 that would be called…

The rest blurred, sliding away before she could visualize the ending. But it was a start. And more than she'd had in a long time.

Holy hell. Where had that come from? Better yet,

could she get more of it if she told Logan to get lost so she could work?

Torn, she eyed him and swore. She'd agreed to do this fake relationship deal, and as she'd been telling herself all week, he had a stake, too. They had places to go and people to let photograph them. Lots of fake kissing to engage in—which she would deny to her grave she looked forward to.

She tapped her temple. "I dare say even I can remember that rule."

Seemed like a dare was pretty close to how she'd gotten him to kiss her the first time.

"Good. We can discuss the rest of the rules on the way. Grab your wrap so we can go."

"Counterproposal. You remember that this is a partnership and I don't answer to you," she shot back. "The whole point is to get eyes on us. This dress is guaranteed to be on a hundred fashion blogs by morning, and to be honest, your love life could use spicing up."

She'd done her homework on Logan McLaughlin, and the mice he normally dated barely registered a blip in the social media sphere. Photographs of him with a woman on his arm were rare in the first place, but the few she'd found—*please*. Either he liked invisible, unassuming women or his vision really *was* impaired.

He crossed his arms. "What's that supposed to mean?"

She almost grinned at his echo of her earlier comment, but only because things were starting to get interesting. Finally. "It means you're boring, darling. One of your players is dating a supermodel who posed for *Playboy*, and he gets more love in the press than anyone else on your team. Take a lesson."

"I'm aware." Logan's back teeth ground together. "I've asked him stop seeing her. It's distasteful."

"Oh, honey." She shook her head. That spine needed unstarching in the worst way, and she definitely had a lot of ideas on how to accomplish *that*. "Thank God you've hooked up with me. Now you listen. We're going to go to this charity deal, I'm not going to wear a wrap and we're going to sizzle. That's the only rule you need."

Logan regretted getting a limo the moment Trinity Forrester spilled into the interior. If he'd driven his own car, he could have occupied himself with the steering wheel. The lack of a place to put his hands hadn't been a factor on the way over. Now? There was entirely too much female skin right there within touching distance.

And God above, the will it took to stop himself from reaching out was monumental.

She smelled both divine and like the kind of sin that would put a man on his knees in a confessional before dawn. The paradox was driving him insane. And they hadn't even pulled away from the curb yet.

A butterfly tattoo flashed at her wrist. It had been covered before, and he was not happy about how much he liked it. He watched as she arranged her long skirt to let her sexy shoes peek out. The heels, of course, resembled ice picks, and only tiny straps held them to her feet, making him wonder how they actually stayed on.

Even her toes were sexy.

"Rules," he growled because he needed some. "Are—"

"Made to be broken?" she filled in sweetly.

The limo shuttled toward what promised to be a very long evening fraught with frustration and tension, most of it sexual, followed by a morning explaining to everyone he knew that he had not, in fact, lost his mind when he'd selected his companion for the evening.

"Rules are necessary so I—we—don't forget what we're doing here." Though he suspected she wasn't dealing with issues in that respect the same way he was. "Without rules, the world descends into chaos."

"Maybe your world does. Mine just gets more interesting."

"Case in point. The most important rule we need to establish is that behind closed doors, we're not a couple. Only in public. And it's not real."

The cockeyed gaze she shot him was further enhanced by her swirly makeup. Less Cleopatra today and more Picasso. It was very distracting.

"I kind of thought all that was a given."

"Well, that's why it's important to lay it out ahead of time. So there's no confusion." That way, there was no end-of-the-evening mix-up at the door where she invited him in for a drink, which was really code for sex, and he'd struggle to remember why he was supposed to say no.

Rules gave him that out.

And really, *this is all fake* was the only rule he needed. She apparently needed a few more, but he'd lost the battle over her outrageous dress and didn't expect he'd win any others—not tonight, anyway. He'd be a hell of lot more specific the next time they appeared in public together.

Rule number two—dress like a woman dating a billionaire who owned a wholesome sports team.

In all actuality, he'd never imagined such a dress existed. Her whole back was bare, dipping low enough to give a guy a tempting glimpse of her rounded bottom. The front wasn't much better, cinching in at the waist to reveal wide panels of her trim waist and abs, and rising over her breasts to cover her to her collarbone. Oddly, the lack of cleavage made his mouth water to unclasp the catch at the back of her neck and let the fabric spill to her hips to reveal the hard nipples tenting the fabric.

He could not get out of this vehicle fast enough.

The limo snaked toward the hotel where the charity ball was being held. When it was their turn to emerge, he got out first and held out a hand to her. He would not have been shocked if she'd refused, but this was it, their first appearance in public together since the kiss clip went viral, and they needed to make it work.

Her hand disappeared into his and he helped her from the limo, happy that she hadn't chosen this moment for their first public fight. Photographers lined the ropes on both sides of the entrance. Instead of beelining for the door like he normally did whenever someone with a camera was around, he paused and slipped an arm around Trinity. His date, for better or worse.

He nearly groaned as his fingertips hit the silky expanse of skin at her hip bone. She might as well be wearing a swimsuit for all the coverage the dress provided. It would take no effort at all to slide his hand inside the fabric and keep going, because there was no way she was wearing underwear. He had the strongest urge to verify.

"Smile," she hissed and snuggled into his embrace far too cozily.

Easy for her to say. She wasn't fighting an erection.

So far, the enormous effort associated with this plan far outweighed the benefit.

A million flashes proved him wrong. More people clamored at the rope than Logan would have ever credited, and every one of them had a lens aimed in his direction. Other couples walked into the building with zero fanfare. Completely ignored.

"Told you this dress would be the ticket," Trinity murmured out of the side of her mouth. "Trust me next time. Kiss me."

"What? Now?"

"What did I just say, Logan?" She smiled up at him, but the curve of her lips was strictly for the audience, because her gaze glittered with challenge. "Don't make me dare you."

He rolled his eyes and laid a chaste kiss on her lips that shouldn't have pumped up the erection in his pants as much as it did. But the score of flashes in his peripheral vision told him her instincts had been dead-on. So he didn't complain. Out loud.

He'd had enough of the spots dancing before his eyes and steered Trinity through the crowd and into the hall, refusing to think about how disappointing that brief kiss had been.

"What is this shindig again?" she asked, eyeing the decorations with enthusiasm.

"It's to benefit Roost, a foundation that helps families relocate and rebuild after a natural disaster. I'm on the board. I took my father's place."

His dad had established the foundation a year before his unexpected death, and Logan had gladly stepped in as the head of the board. It meant something to him to continue Duncan McLaughlin's legacy.

Of course the real heroes were the people doing the heavy lifting; Logan just funneled money into the coffers and ensured Roost's logo appeared regularly during baseball games. Occasionally, he showed up at a fancy deal like this one and gave a speech.

Her gaze cut to him and held far more appreciation than it should. "I've heard of Roost. I didn't know you were involved in it. It's a cause you're passionate about or is this just a family obligation?"

The offhand question dug at him, tripping more than a few wires inside. "Why can't it be both?"

She shrugged one bare shoulder. "I guess it can be. Just seems to me that if you're going to champion a cause, it should be your own. Not your father's."

"My father was my role model. I would do well to emulate him. So would a lot of people."

"Of course." But he didn't mistake her comment as agreement, and it did nothing to cool his suddenly boiling temper. "And you'd also do well to be yourself instead of a carbon copy of someone else. A philosophy you might guess I readily subscribe to."

A lecture on individuality from the woman with a tongue piercing was not on the agenda for the evening. Neither was a dissection of his desire to follow in his father's footsteps. "I'm happy with who I am, thanks. Roost is important to me. Have you seen what a house looks like after a tornado tears through it? It's my pleasure to drum up support for people who have lost everything."

"I'll write you a check later," she murmured as several people picked that moment to ask for an introduction to his date. "It's the least I can do."

"You're already doing the least you can," he commented under his breath and dived into the social minutiae required at such an event before she could come up with what would no doubt be a cutting rebuttal.

It was nice to win one occasionally.

Trinity chatted up the curious guests with ease, clearly in her element, while Logan thought seriously about leaving early. Wearing a tux ranked about last on his list of fun things to do, followed shortly by eating in a formal setting. As a member of the board, he had the dubious privilege of being seated at the head table, where all eyes stayed trained on him and his flashy date.

His uncomfortable awareness of her dimmed not at all as they worked their way through steak and asparagus that probably tasted great when it wasn't flavored by visions of whirling a woman into the shadows to see just how naked she was under that dress.

When the band struck up a slow jazz number, Trinity's hand snaked beneath the table to squeeze his thigh. He avoided jumping like a teenager, but just barely.

"What?" he muttered.

"Ask me to dance, ding-dong," she shot back in a whisper.

He checked his ninth or tenth eye roll of the evening and stood to offer her his hand. "Would you do me the honor, Ms. Forrester?"

She didn't bother to check her own eye roll as she let him help her to her feet. "Are you trying to sound ninety, or does it come automatically?"

"I never come automatically." He cursed. That had slipped out and probably told her far too much about his mental state.

"I'll keep that in mind." She sounded like she was trying not to laugh.

They walked out on the dance floor and his hands drifted into place at her waist as if he'd done it a thousand times. Which, theoretically, he had—if you counted all the times he'd done it in his mind since opening the door earlier that evening.

She felt so good that his fingers spread across her skin without any prompting on his part, but he couldn't help wanting more contact. The point was to give the appearance that they were into each other. He just wished it wasn't so easy to fake that part.

Unlike earlier, no crush of cameras clamored to capture their every move, but there were still plenty of eyes on them, which meant they had to make it look good. It helped that she moved in sync with him as they danced, a shocking turn of events. If anything, he'd have expected her to try to lead, to boss him around—anything other than the fluidity they fell into instantly, as if they'd danced before.

She peered up at him from under her lashes and smiled, which hit him with the approximate force of a fighter jet at Mach 5. Apparently she wasn't on board with the respectable distance he'd put between them, because she scooted closer, deliberately brushing his body with hers as she swayed.

It took far too long to unstick his tongue from the roof of his mouth. He was thirty-five years old, for crying out loud, and had certainly bedded a few hot women. Of course that had been a fair number of years ago, before he started looking for the future Mrs. McLaughlin.

"So," he said inanely. "Here we are."

One of the pitfalls of a fake relationship—they had to pretend they actually had things to talk about.

"Mmm, yes, we are here," she agreed easily.

Her hands meandered under his tux jacket to cup his butt, which she then fingered suggestively. Every drop of blood in his body drained into his groin, and his brain fuzzed.

"Um, what are you doing?" he choked out. "Are there cameras on us that I can't see?"

"Nope. I'm just naturally handsy. And curious." Her blue eyes glowed in the low ballroom light. "How can

I fake being hot and heavy with you if I don't actually know what your butt feels like when I grab it?"

He groaned as he envisioned the scenario under which she might be grabbing his butt—as she cried his name in her throaty voice, urging him on as he drove her to a blistering climax, for example. Or maybe as he pinned her to the wall and took her standing up. Or, his personal favorite, as she knelt before him and pleasured him with her hot mouth, sliding that tongue piercing across his flesh.

His vision grayed for a second, and he might have lost the feeling in his legs.

"Do I get the same courtesy?" he muttered, thoroughly impressed with himself that he wasn't laid out on the floor. "Because there's a lot of you I haven't grabbed yet, either."

They were so close, her laugh vibrated through his tight groin.

"What are you going to do if I say yes?"

"This." It was close enough to a dare that he locked gazes with her and slid two fingers under the fabric of her dress to caress one bare globe of her rounded bottom. No panties, as he'd guessed.

The temperature shot up as heat flushed through his body.

And then it was no longer a point to be proven, but an exploration of the woman he'd been angling to get his hands on all night.

God, she felt amazing, like warm silk. Heat flared in her expression, winnowing through his blood until he couldn't stop himself from pressing closer, desperately seeking more of her, questing for relief from the needy ache she'd induced.

"I don't recall actually saying yes," she said. Instantly he withdrew, a millisecond from spitting out an apology, when she grinned. "But I wasn't saying no, either."

"Make up your mind, woman," he growled.

"I'm not the one who laid down the ground rules. Wasn't there something about none of this being real?" She shimmied her hips in a practiced rhythm against his painful erection. "That feels pretty real to me. Are you sure *I'm* the one who can't make up her mind?"

She'd baited him on purpose. Probably had deliberately worn this dress with the easily accessible butt cheeks to drive him insane. This was exactly the reason he should have said no to this ridiculous fake relationship. Trinity Forrester was too bold, too exotic, too… *sensual* for a man who just wanted a nice girl to come home to at the end of a long day.

Nice girls didn't constantly make him think about getting naked.

"Why do you have to make everything about sex?" he grumbled. "Can't we just dance?"

And now he sounded exactly like what she'd accused him of: a Goody Two-shoes. A ninety-year-old. A stickler for rules.

That was not who he was. This woman had been manipulating him all night, and he was done with it. He'd agreed to this fake relationship but he hadn't agreed to let her run roughshod over him.

That stopped now.

"Me?" She had the audacity to feign surprise. "I've never so much as uttered the word *sex* one time."

"You don't have to. It wafts from your pores." Eyes narrowed, he spun her around until he could dance her off the marble floor and into the shadows at the back of the room.

She had reasons for why she was so overtly sexy, so in-your-face with her asymmetrical hair and tongue piercing, and none of them were because she was a free spirit who reveled in her individuality.

She was hiding something behind her shock value.

Let's just see how you handle a man who has your number, Ms. Forrester.

Before she could blink, he had her trapped against the wall, his body pressing hard against hers. Exactly where he wanted to be, every nerve primed to sink into her.

More than that…he wanted to expose her secrets in the same way she'd peeled back his need to be like his father.

"Cameras?" She peered around his shoulder in anticipation.

"No idea." He tipped up her chin, guiding her attention back where it belonged. "I'm just curious about whether kissing you feels as good as I remember."

Her expression heated as she zeroed in on him, ignoring the crowd. "Well, that doesn't sound like it's in the rules according to Logan."

"It's number three," he corrected silkily. "When a woman has been begging you for something all night, you give it to her."

And exactly like the first time he'd kissed her, he couldn't stop himself from caving to the blinding need to have her mouth under his. Their lips connected, and instantly, he parted hers to savagely seek her taste.

It exploded on his tongue. Back and forth, give and take, he kissed her with every ounce of pent-up longing and passion and frustration that he'd been battling since the moment she'd slid into his limo. Since before that. Since that first kiss.

He wanted to strip her raw and tunnel under her outrageous appeal in hopes of tempering it somehow.

The cool hardness of the steel rod through her tongue skated along his hot tongue, and yes, the contrast and the sheer uniqueness of the sensation was as affecting as he remembered. More so. Because there were no cameras on them this time and he didn't have to think about decorum if he didn't feel like it.

He didn't feel like it.

They'd be so hot together. He wouldn't have to think about anything but pleasure. She'd tell him what she wanted, take it, give it back tenfold, and there'd be nothing but miles of skin and Trinity's laugh.

Her hands were everywhere, in his hair and caressing his face, against his back.

He returned the favor, groaning deep in his chest as he slid both hands beneath the fabric of her dress to take as much of her bare bottom into his palms as would fit. Which wasn't much, because the stupid wall was in the way. He eased up his full-body press enough to go deeper, and that got a moan out of her that was like music to his ears.

"You're stopping," she murmured. "Don't stop."

He groaned. Again. Oh, yes, it would be so easy to wedge his hand between her legs and continue his exploration of the secrets under that dress. But they were in public, with other couples taking advantage of the shadows a mere few feet away.

He'd never been so tempted to throw caution to the wind.

"If I touch you like that, I want to be someplace where you don't have to be quiet," he advised her. His name tearing from her throat as she came over and over again would be perfect.

She smiled and nipped at his lips with hers, rolling her hips against his erection. "Trust me when I say I have a lot of practice letting a man pleasure me in places where noise isn't kosher."

He sucked in a breath. He so did not need to hear that. Too late. His mind started filling in the blanks, calculating how wild and insane an affair he and Trinity could actually indulge in and still stick to the rules—after all, they weren't behind closed doors.

His body nearly made the decision for him, straining toward her in eager anticipation.

No. He had more control than this. He could not let her drag him under her spell. No matter how slick and ready she must be. No matter how much he ached to find out if she was as turned on as he was. "You've never done that with me. I seriously doubt you could keep it together."

"Only one way to find out."

"That's not going to work this time." He shook his head. The only reason it wouldn't was because he seriously feared that if he gave in, she'd suck him so far down into her bad-girl fantasy that he wouldn't ever be able to cut himself free.

And he needed to be disentangled if he ever hoped to find something real.

Four

The sketches refused to come together.

Trinity threw down her pencil and let her head drop into her hands. A whole Saturday wasted on the premise of the ad campaign she'd glimpsed in her mind while with Logan last night. Wisps of it had floated through her consciousness while they'd been dancing. Then when he'd kissed her—it was like her entire body had woken up from a hundred-year sleep.

Glorious, wonderful inspiration flowed like lava. And then the man had flooded her, pushing out everything but him as he lit her up with his mouth. His hands had done a good job igniting sparks, too.

When he forgot to be a stick in the mud, Logan McLaughlin set her on fire.

Coaxing him out of his all-American shell had become somewhat of a favorite pastime. She hadn't gotten him there yet, not all the way, but he'd veered much farther toward the dark side than she'd have expected.

No more fantasies about teaching him everything she knew.

Back to work.

Instead of beating her head against the brick wall of her creativity, she checked a few of her social media accounts, where she'd reposted several of the better pictures from last night. A few shares. Nothing had gone viral like the video from the show. Of course, the majority of the photos circulating this morning were the posed ones in front of the limo where she'd practically had to order Logan to kiss her. The pictures were nice. Sweet. Not enough to generate a buzz in her stomach, so she held little hope they would generate much of a buzz with the public, either.

If only someone had captured Logan's hand down her dress as he kissed her within an iota of stripping her naked—*that* would have burned up the web. But alas, no one with a camera had been in shooting distance of those shadows, apparently. Shame. They'd have to do better next time, be more deliberate about their choice of locales.

Shadows.

What if... She picked up her pencil and sketched a quick drawing of two silhouettes engaged in a very hot kiss. Ad copy could go something like, *With Formula-47, you don't have to stay in the shadows. Because it fixes your scars.*

Eh. That wasn't exactly award-winning stuff, especially if she had to explain the concept. If only she could come up with a name, the rest would definitely fall into place. She had until Monday. And then the only things that would fall if she didn't have her act together were the faces of her friends and business partners, who were expecting a marketing presentation designed to sell the living daylights out of their signature product.

So, this was not helping. Maybe if she could generate a better showing for her brand-new fake relationship, some of the pressure would be off and her muse
would get with the program.

Palming her phone, she sent Logan a text message
asking if he was free tonight before the little voices
could start laughing at her feeble attempts to make ex-
cuses for wanting to see him. Yeah, she'd had fun last
night after figuring out that the key to everything was
getting him hot and bothered. It wasn't a crime to admit
she'd rather press those buttons than sit here failing at
being brilliant for the rest of her Saturday.

The return message came back instantly.

It's the ninth inning, so I can jet in a couple of hours.
What did you have in mind?

Crap. Should have thought that through a little better. What she had in mind and what was feasible to
actually do in a crowd were two different things, despite what she'd told Logan last night about her public
exploits. But it was only fair that she come up with an
event since he'd done the work last night.

Something that didn't require hours to get ready
would be great. And necessary, since it was already
four o'clock. Something public, where she could goad
him into a fight, preferably, because that seemed to have
worked the first time to get so many shares.

Nada.

It wasn't like she never did social stuff. But for so
long, she'd done them with her friends, met interesting
men wherever they ended up, and then gone home with
one if she was in the mood. Or not, as the case had been

lately. And her friends had all gotten married, leaving her at loose ends and restless.

Married friends might be a saving grace right this minute.

There was nothing to do but ping Cass and ask if she and Gage were by some miracle in Dallas today instead of Austin and if they had plans. Maybe the CEO of Fyra might be up for a double date, and there would be the added benefit of having two more social powerhouses with her, since both Cass and Gage regularly made the society columns in both of the cities they frequented.

Cass texted her back almost immediately.

We have invitations to a party in Deep Ellum to benefit Children's Advocacy Center, but we're skipping due to all the smoke and loud music. Baby on board, as Gage likes to remind me. You want to go in our place?

Trinity did a victory dance. Looked like she'd be taking Logan to a club after all, and the timing was perfect. She texted him to pick her up at eight, then shut her laptop lid so she didn't have to stare at the blank screen any longer.

Humming, she took a shower, then did her makeup. Harper had just come up with a really great new eye shadow that she'd asked everyone to test. The deep emerald color matched Trinity's mood and had a touch of sparkle, perfect for a dark venue. She poured herself into a faux leather catsuit in black with a silver chain ring belt and donned six-inch platform heels that complemented the outfit but didn't totally scream *dominatrix*.

Logan's expression when she opened the door later said that he didn't quite get the distinction.

"No." He shook his head and shut his eyes for a beat. "I'm not going anywhere with you dressed like a cross between Catwoman and Lady Gaga."

That was such a ludicrous statement, she actually glanced down. "Are you kidding? Lady Gaga would laugh at how tame these shoes are. Also, we're not having this argument every time, are we?"

"Apparently." He crossed his arms over his Dallas Mustangs T-shirt, bunching up his biceps in the way that drove her mad. Because she still hadn't gotten her hands on them, not properly. "Until you get the memo that I'm a conservative, God-fearing baseball team owner who sells hot dogs, foam fingers and memories, not bondage equipment."

"Honey, you're about as conservative as a Ferrari." And twice as sexy. He was a little windblown, as if he'd driven from the stadium in Arlington with the windows open. "No one who kisses a woman like you do could ever be described as tame."

Windblown Logan was delicious. Almost as much as tuxedo-clad Logan. Maybe more. The tux had lent him an almost inaccessible air, too beautiful to mar, but today he had a ready-to-rumble look that said he'd throw down if she pushed. And she was in the mood to push.

"Tame and conservative are not the same thing," he said with a once-over that had enough bite that her lady parts perked up. "Kissing you directly benefits my goals. You wearing that outfit does not."

She crossed her arms to mimic him and let a slow smile spill over her face. "I'm not changing. We're going to a club in Deep Ellum. I guarantee you I will blend in. You won't."

"Good. Then we'll attract more attention if we don't blend." Without asking, he barged into her condo like a bull with the red cape in his sights, then whirled in the marble entryway. "Which direction is your bedroom?"

"Well, if I'd known that's all it took to get you there, I'd have worn this outfit the first day."

He scowled. "Stop being dense. You're wearing different clothes. I need to find your closet."

"Oh, that's a terrible reason to be in a woman's bedroom. Just curious, are you going to wrestle me out of this outfit?" Leaning on the open door frame, she contemplated him and pointed down the hall. "Because if the answer's yes, my bedroom is that way."

"Fantastic."

And then, without any warning, he swung her up into his arms as if she weighed no more than a child, slammed the door shut with his foot and carried her to her bedroom. Her pulse tripled as the hard planes of his torso cradled her body. God, he was as solid and strong as she'd always imagined, but he held her gently, as if he didn't want to break her. If she hadn't already been snuggled into his embrace, her weak knees might have put her on the floor.

Even though she knew he'd only done it to avoid the rest of the argument, the gesture was so…gallant. As many men as had crossed her threshold, not one had ever treated her like she was delicate, and honestly, she'd have shown every last one of them the door if they had.

There was something about Logan and his old-fashioned streak that hit her between the eyes, almost as if he refused to see her as a sex object, no matter how she regarded herself. It shouldn't be so affecting. But there it was.

He deposited her on the bed without a word and strode to her closet, throwing wide the doors without hesitation, as if he'd dressed many a woman in his day. And maybe he had.

Oh, hell. She kind of wanted to see what he'd pick out.

"Here." He came out of the closet with a pair of 7 for All Mankind jeans and a simple black T-shirt that she wore to spin class sometimes. "Put this on."

She couldn't help it. She laughed. "So we can be twins?"

He threw the clothes on the bed and hunted around in her drawers until he found a bra and panties, both black, which was an interesting attention to detail she appreciated, completely against her will. When was the last time a man paid *that* much attention to her?

Handing her the undergarments, he stared down at her on the bed. "No. So I can see the real you underneath all of your deflections."

The earnestness in his expression froze her lungs and dried up every scrap of amusement in this situation. "What do you mean, the real me? This is as real as I get."

Before she could move, breathe, blink, he knelt on the bed and grabbed one foot, slowly unbuckling her platform sandal. Transfixed, she watched, too curious where he was headed to stop him.

"In public, it's not real. Behind closed doors, we're not anything but two people who don't know each other. All bets are off. I want to see what you're hiding underneath all of this outlandishness."

Oh, God. He was serious. And so intent that it bobbled her pulse. But she was nothing if not voraciously attracted to new experiences. What was the worst thing that could happen? Her pulse thumped as he tossed the first shoe over his shoulder. His gorgeous hazel eyes did not have an ounce of hesitation in them.

"By all means, strip away." She granted him permission to continue with a wave of her hand as if it didn't matter, but that would be a lie.

This was far from the first time a man had undressed her. But the way he was doing it tripped a hundred sensors in her chest, warning her it wasn't going to be like any of those other times.

Despite the heavy awareness spreading across her skin, this wasn't about sex, and neither of them was confused about that. It was about something else. A quest for knowledge.

She'd always considered herself an open book, but as he dropped the other shoe to her hardwood floor, she suddenly wondered if he'd sense all the dark and personal corners of herself that she'd never shared with anyone.

The brokenness inside wasn't something she liked to think about.

And that made her want to slam the book shut.

But it was too late. He peeled the catsuit from her shoulders and dragged it to her waist, his gaze locked on to hers, never straying to the skin he was revealing. Somehow, that made the act of him undressing her *more* sensuous.

She'd expected him to look, to ogle her naked body, because come on. He *was* a man, as red-blooded as any she'd ever met, and he had pulled out a bra and panties. He knew she didn't have anything on under this outfit.

Carefully, he lifted her hips and kept going, unwrapping her so slowly that her throat burned. When she twisted to release the fabric from under her legs, his fingertips grazed the brilliant green ivy tattoo twining around her thigh. She could feel the question in his touch, and her muscles quivered.

"It leads to the garden of Eden," she murmured as he laid her bodysuit aside. "Or so the story goes."

His gaze cut to her eyes.

"What's the real story?" he asked quietly. Unobtrusively. Sincerely, as if he really did want to know who she was.

"Ivy is hearty. It climbs. The vine grows little feet and will cling to almost any surface until it's taller than the structure it's climbing on. That resonates with me."

"You're tenacious." He nodded and slid the panties over her legs and trailed his thumb across the tattoo as he settled them into place. "That's a good quality."

She shrugged, mystified why he'd picked that word from the concept she'd thrown out. She'd always thought of it as survival and then domination of her surroundings, because it was that or be trampled underfoot. Ivy was one of those plants that when you stumbled over ruins, it would still be thriving. Maybe even overtaking the entire structure.

The butterfly tattoo on her wrist had meaning to her as well. Everything she'd done to decorate her body had significance. She wasn't sure how much she liked that he'd immediately dug that out of her.

His thumb continued stroking her thigh, and she got very aware of his hands on her very fast. "Your thumb is a little low. The garden is underneath those panties you just put on me."

"Are you asking me to touch you?" His voice was rough with a need that thrilled her. "Because that is very against the rules."

"Make some new ones," she said and let the challenge roll through the space between them, of which there was way too much for her taste. Maybe this hadn't been about sex at the start, but it could be now. It *should* be. "I'm just going to ignore them all anyway. I'm very good at being bad."

To demonstrate, she slid her fingertips up his leg to brush his groin, but just as she was about to curl her palm around his shaft, he grabbed her hand, removing it forcibly.

"Why do you do that?" he said point-blank, holding her hand in his as far away from his body as he could.

"Do what?" She stared at him, desperately trying to figure out where she'd miscalculated. He wanted her, and there was no way he could lie about it when she'd felt the evidence herself. "Refuse to pull punches when I want something? I'm not going to apologize. I like sex."

"No, you don't. You like control, and seduction is how you get it." He stared right back. "It amuses you to lead a man around, and sex keeps him occupied so he doesn't dig too far down into places he's not welcome."

Shock made her hand go limp. "I don't do that."

She did. She so did.

How the hell had he figured that out when they hadn't even slept together yet?

"You do. You flirt and wear outrageous clothes and advertise your availability purely as a distraction. What are you afraid I'm going to find out?"

That she longed to be the kind of woman a man wanted to stay with. Since she wasn't, she might as well get something out of a man's company. Orgasms worked for her.

She tossed her hair. "I'm not the one who's afraid, McLaughlin. It bothers you that you're so attracted to me. That's why you want me in boring clothes, so you can keep pretending you don't have a secret desire to do all sorts of wicked things to me. Things you know I'd like. You're throwing all of this in my face because you're the one who needs a distraction. Stop being such a Goody Two-shoes and take what you want."

"What I want is for you to put these clothes on so we can go." The catch in his voice said he wasn't as unaffected as he'd like her to believe. "Good sex stems from intimacy. Connection. I like to have that with someone I'm sleeping with."

I want to see the real you.

He'd meant it. That hadn't been a ploy to get her out of an outfit he'd hated.

And all at once, she wanted to give it to him. To have this thing between them be real. She could confess all her secrets, tell him how he made her feel feminine for the first time in a long time. He wouldn't care that she couldn't have babies; he'd like her for her.

They'd have something between them besides sex.

That's when her fantasy dried up and blew away. What did she know about how to be in a real relationship? Nothing, obviously, or she'd have figured out how to keep Neil around once she'd told him she'd conceived.

Dutifully, she let Logan hook her bra into place and raised her arms so he could pull the T-shirt over her head, suddenly grateful for the cover. She felt oddly exposed, as if the sheer act of informing her that he was stripping away her shields along with her outfit could actually accomplish it.

And she had enough appreciation for the psychology behind his assessment to be a little freaked that he'd come up with such a tactic. Enough that she let him pull her from the bed so he could slide her jeans over her hips and then button them, fully concealing her. It marked the first time in her life that a man had dressed her, only for her to wind up more naked than when she'd worn nothing.

The appreciation shining in Logan's eyes as he laced his fingers with hers put a different kind of heat low in her belly. This barely-make-a-blip outfit had more effect than the in-your-face sexy one. For Logan, at least. What was she supposed to *do* with him?

"You're a beautiful woman, Trinity." He stated it like a fact, but that didn't decrease the potency in the slightest. "Dressed like this, you make so much more of an impact, because it allows you to be the star instead of the outfit."

Her knees did go weak at that, but she locked them. Now was not the time to get mushy over Logan McLaughlin. No time was good for that. This was all fake and designed to go his way so he could control his image. Nothing more.

She had to remember the most important rule— none of this was real. That was the reason he hadn't undressed her and used it as an excuse to cop a feel or ogle her. He wasn't attracted to her other than at a base level, and only then because it was involuntary physiology, not the connection he was looking for.

Good. She didn't want that. Not with Logan, not with any man.

Except maybe she did, and she did not like that he'd uncovered a longing she'd had no idea was there. A longing she had no business indulging in, because she didn't work like other women, couldn't. Her body wasn't made for pregnancy, and her ability to trust the opposite gender didn't exist. She had to stop this nonsense cold.

"Maybe I like my clothes to be the star," she muttered, and to her mortification, tears pricked at her eyelids. What in the hell was this man doing to her?

A better question was, why was she letting him?

"Wearing this outfit will get us the top spot on people's social media feeds, I guarantee it," he said mildly. "Do me one last favor and wear the shoes, though. I like it when you're tall enough for me to put my arm around you."

Oh, really?

The tears coupled with the unexpected exposure and longings that shouldn't even be a factor put her in a dangerous mood. "I call BS. You like these shoes because you have secret bad-girl fantasies."

He rolled his eyes. "It's not a stretch to say I like sexy shoes on a woman. I readily admit to that."

That set her back. The man was honest to a fault, and it kept throwing her off. He was supposed to lie to her and act like an ass and pull immature ghosting routines where he pretended his phone was off when she tried to reach him.

Maybe he'd already lied to her. Like when he said he wanted intimacy instead of sex. Or was he actually lying to himself about what he wanted?

"If I wear the shoes," she murmured throatily, "do I get a reward?"

Suspicion clouded his expression. "Like what? A gold star?"

She shrugged. "Maybe you take me to the bathroom in the club and see how far your hand goes down these jeans. Or didn't you notice how tiny these panties are on me?"

"I noticed," he said shortly and ran a hand through his hair, a habit she'd started to clue in meant he felt uncomfortable. "Trust me, I'm not that much of a good guy."

News to her. "Tell me. Would it be so bad to let your bad boy out to play occasionally?"

His eyes narrowed. "Yes, it would."

When he didn't elaborate, her curiosity went through

the roof. So he wasn't denying that he had a wild streak. Interesting. Because if he had denied it, she'd have called him on that, too. No man who put his hands down a woman's dress in a crowded ballroom with scarcely a glance around could claim he'd never done anything like that before.

Seemed like Logan might be hiding behind his public persona, too. What would he be like if she stripped him of his conservative armor?

Suddenly, she was ready to get him out in public, where she could flirt and seduce and provoke him into putting his hands on her again without fear. Because behind closed doors, it wasn't real. She had to get out of here before she forgot they weren't a couple with an interest in getting to know each other beneath the surface.

By ten o'clock, Logan had a pounding headache that beat against his temples in perfect time to the garbage being pumped out of the speakers at the Deep Ellum club Trinity had dragged him to.

The Mustangs had lost today—again—and what he should really be doing was combing through his roster—again—to see where he could make improvements.

As a whole, the team's manager had point on the fine details, but he had to work with the talent Logan gave him. It was the general manager's job to get the right guys onto the field for the best price. Bang for the buck was key when it came to the financials of a ball team. Managing money should come easily considering his DNA, but it didn't. He had to work at it.

So instead of crunching numbers and looking at possible trade angles, Logan leaned against the bar nursing a light beer that wasn't fit for unclogging a drain. The view was nice, though. Trinity perched on a bar stool, clutching a highball, one jeans-clad leg entwined with his. She'd done that a while back in a seriously sexy *back off, ladies* move that had raised his eyebrows, but he kind of loved it.

They couldn't exactly talk due to the music, yet the contact created a sense of intimacy he'd never have expected. As a result, he'd been sporting a semi in his pants since the moment her leg had snaked possessively around his.

All right, the fact that she was wearing jeans and a T-shirt that he'd personally put on her body might have a little more to do with the hard-on. When he'd said he wanted to see the real her, he hadn't expected to like it so much, or to discover a burning desire to uncover more. He'd barely scratched the surface of what lay beneath Trinity's outrageous exterior. And that thirst for knowledge was at least 50 percent of the reason he was still here.

The bump in ticket sales was the other fifty. Myra couldn't control her glee earlier when she'd phoned him in the dugout to say that today's game had hit an all-time high for attendance. Which unfortunately wasn't saying much, but it was saying *something*.

There was definitely room to get some more press, though.

And he needed to do it before his skull split in two.

A photographer had been circulating near the front of the club, and he bided his time until he saw her headed toward the bar. From the corner of his eye, he tracked her progress until she was close enough to guarantee she wouldn't miss it if he tossed her a great shot.

Logan plucked the highball from Trinity's grasp. Before she could squawk, he swiveled her stool and cupped her face in both hands, bringing it up to his. Their lips connected.

It should have been a token kiss, just show. But this was Trinity, and she didn't hesitate to open her mouth. That steel piercing slid hard across his tongue, sensitizing him all the way to the bottoms of his feet. Her arms raced down his back. She flattened her palms against it and shoved, grinding his erection straight into her center, hard enough to put stars across his vision.

God, yes, more of that. Aching, fiery need exploded between them, and he wrapped a hand around her thigh dangerously close to the ivy tattoo under her jeans, hauling her leg higher on his hip. The angle opened her wider and the stool was just the right height to make everything feel unbelievably good.

Deepening the kiss shouldn't have been so effortless, but she was as into it as he was, her moans vibrating her chest against his, or maybe that was the thump of the bass jarring them both. Whatever it was, this was the hottest kiss he'd ever participated in.

The music wasn't loud enough to cover the hoots of the surrounding partygoers, though, and somehow it filtered through his head that he'd more than accomplished his goal of laying a photo-worthy kiss on his date. And publicity was the only reason to be doing it. The only logical reason, anyway, and the only one he'd admit to.

With far more reluctance than he'd like, he ended the kiss and pulled away, but Trinity was having none of that. She threaded her fingers through his hair, pressed against his neck and nuzzled his nose with hers, brushing their lips together, and suddenly they were kissing again.

But this time, it was a slow slide into an intense web of awareness. Everything faded and time stopped as he tasted heaven. The floodgates of his body opened, welcoming her in. This was connection, the kind he'd said he wanted. It was so much more than a kiss, and he craved it like he craved blood to his heart.

This was what it was like to kiss the woman behind the curtain. No barriers. He'd been looking for the essence of Trinity and he'd found it. More importantly, she'd given it to him. It spread through him, warm, thick, sweet, and it was so right that it became a part of him instantly, as if she had always been there.

One of her hot hands slipped under the hem of his shirt, scrabbling at his waist as if she'd slide off the stool if she didn't hold on. He totally understood that. Because he was careening down a slippery slope as well, hitting a hundred miles an hour with no brakes.

And that's what finally snapped him out of it.

When he'd told her he wanted intimacy, he'd expected her to balk. It was supposed to put another barrier between them, a reminder that he wanted a home and hearth kind of woman, not one who threatened to incinerate every bone in his body.

This time, when he pulled back, she let him go, her arms falling into her lap. She blinked, reorienting herself, apparently as befuddled as he was by what had just happened.

"Did she get the shot?" Trinity murmured, and instantly it was business as usual.

"She better have."

If not, he was done with this farce. There was no way he could keep this up. Because it was starting to feel way too real even when they weren't behind closed doors.

When Logan's phone rang at 8:00 a.m., *Mom* was the last name he expected to see flashing on the screen.

He groaned and put a pillow over his head, but it still felt like each chime of the ringtone cut straight through his temples. He knocked the phone onto the bed without looking and dragged it under the pillow. "Don't you have church?"

"Hello to you, too." His mother was way too chipper for a Sunday morning. "I'm about to leave, yes. You should come with me."

"I have a game today," he reminded her, which she should know, since she had box seats and came to most home games. When he was free, he didn't mind taking his mom to the church she'd attended with his dad for over thirty years. He hated that she had to go by herself now.

"Judging by the pictures your grandmother forwarded me, you'd do better to come with me to church," his mother said and he could hear her raised eyebrows in her tone. "Who is this woman you were kissing like you wanted to swallow her whole?"

"Trinity Forrester." He could not have this conversation at 8:00 a.m. on a Sunday. Or any time on any day, for that matter. How did he live in a world where Grandma got her mitts on photos posted to the internet and tattled to his mother about them? "And it was just a kiss."

It was so not just a kiss, and odds were the photographer had captured the scene at the club last night at the height of the frenzy. Logan hadn't seen the pictures yet, but they must have been really good if they warranted an early-morning call regarding the subject of his eternal soul.

"Would it be too much to ask if I could meet her? Since you're seriously involved and everything?"

Logan groaned. "Mom, I'm not marrying her. We're just...dating."

"That's not what the caption says."

He sat up, knocking the pillow to the floor. "What? What does it say?"

"'Billionaire owner of the Dallas Mustangs celebrates as Fyra Cosmetics executive says yes to his proposal.'" She cleared her throat. "That's verbatim. I'm reading it straight off my screen."

Since he didn't need any more invitations to church, he bit back an inventive curse. "It's...complicated, Mom."

He couldn't flat-out deny it, not until he knew if Trinity had planted the story on purpose. She better not have. He'd already told her his views on a fake engagement. His temper set off at a slow boil.

"Oh. So are you engaged or not?"

He couldn't lie to his mom, either. They'd always been close, but since his dad had died, Logan made sure that his mom wanted for nothing. They'd made the agonizing decision together to sell McLaughlin Investments, the online stock trading company his dad had founded, and then split the money in half. It had bonded them in a way nothing else could have. "I'll call you later and tell you. How about that?"

"As long as the answer is yes, sure."

Of course that was what she'd say. She'd been bemoaning the lack of a daughter-in-law for going on ten years now and recently had started in on the lack of grandchildren. *You're not getting any younger*, she liked to remind him, *and I'm certainly not.*

He had a ticking clock in his head, too, and didn't need any help feeling like the life full of family and kids that he saw when he closed his eyes did not even slightly resemble the one he lived every day. The line of eligible women wrapped the block twice, but he couldn't seem to find the *right* future Ms. McLaughlin. Certainly he would not increase his chances by parading a fake one around.

A shower did not improve his mood, and neither did the images that had been flashing across his mind since the undressing of last night. Trinity's body was the stuff of legends, and he was not the nice guy she'd painted him as.

Oddly, thinking about that second kiss put more wood in his shed than visualizing her perfect breasts as he peeled off that outfit made of sofa cushion material. So horrible. But once it was gone? So beautiful.

The woman. The kiss. The way she'd made herself vulnerable to him, both on that bed as he'd stripped away all of the outer trappings that hid Trinity from the world and on that bar stool as he explored what he'd found. So amazing.

He palmed himself and took care of the worst of the aching need, but he suspected he wouldn't ever fully absolve it until he gave in to the inevitable.

Which wasn't happening.

When he got out of the shower, he hunted up something to eat in the enormous kitchen that had come with the house he'd bought in Prosper because it was close to the Mustangs training facility and the school district was one of the best in north Texas.

Yeah, it had occurred to him that the woman he eventually married might like to pick out her own house, but he'd fallen in love with the property the moment his Realtor showed it to him. Twenty rolling acres spread out around the main house with plenty of room for kids and dogs, and a stable sat up on a hill overlooking a lake that he'd stocked with fish. Now all he needed was the wife.

Apparently he'd been granted step one in that process without his consent, and since he really couldn't put it off any longer, Logan snatched his laptop from the built-in desk near the fireplace in the great room and booted it up as he mainlined coffee.

The shot spilled onto his screen, and yeah, it was hot. He was standing between Trinity's legs, back to the camera and his hand on her thigh. The photographer had captured the kiss perfectly to show Trinity's face and expression—rapturous.

Logan's entire body cued up at the memory. This wasn't a picture of two people faking it for the camera. They wanted each other more than they wanted to breathe, and it was all there in full color for the world to see.

That's what his mom should be worried about, not whether the caption had any validity, although it did say exactly what she'd said it did.

Trinity Forrester was not the woman of his dreams. Fantasies? Sure. It would be impossible not to think about finishing that kiss with all her clothes on the floor. But the idea of her being his fake fiancée did not sit well. At all. He needed to call her, but it was barely nine o'clock on a Sunday and despite all of the evidence burning up his laptop screen, he did have a small sense of decorum left.

His phone beeped with a text message from none other.

Looked like she wasn't a late sleeper, either.

Did you see? It's all over my social media. I need a ring.

That pushed far more buttons than he should have allowed, and his temper flared. A fake relationship was one thing, because frankly, it wasn't all that fake. They *were* dating, and no one had asked how serious it was, so there had been no reason to lie. Until today.

He called her. Some things couldn't be properly conveyed via text message.

"Isn't it great?" she gushed by way of answer. Clearly she'd been sitting on her phone waiting on a return text and was perfectly fine with a conversation instead. "My publicist already called me. She's thrilled with the response. One of her trackers says the picture with the proposal caption has been shared twenty-five thousand times."

The phone nearly slipped from his suddenly nerveless fingers.

"Twenty-five thousand? Really?"

God, the nightmare just kept going, didn't it? How was it possible that people cared so much about something as unimportant to their daily lives as two people they'd never met getting engaged? And it was a lie, besides.

"That's just the one with your hand on my thigh. The other one is better, but it's not getting as much traction, probably because it's not as splashy."

The other one? Wedging his phone against his ear, he did another search and so many results scrolled onto his screen, he could hardly fathom it. There. He clicked.

The photographer had gotten a one-in-a-million shot in that moment after Logan had pulled away, in between the first and second kisses, just as Trinity had started to reel him back in. They weren't kissing, not yet, but the raw desire on her face was unmistakable. This picture was worth a thousand words, perfectly encapsulating what he'd felt as he'd been sucked into her—as if flesh and bone had dissolved, leaving only their essence behind.

She'd felt it, too. And he hated sharing what should have been a private moment with the world.

He hated a lot of this.

"I'm not buying you a ring," he muttered. "Are you the one who planted that caption?"

"No, I was just as surprised as you were. It might have been my publicist, but she won't admit it."

"We have to set the record straight. That's nonnegotiable. I don't mind letting a bunch of strangers think we're dating, but it's not fair to the people in my life to let them think there might be a wedding in our future when there's not."

"Why do we have to say anything?" She waved off all of his concern with that one airy statement. "No one is asking for an interview. Let it ride. See how your numbers are Monday morning and then let's strategize some more."

Easy for her to say. If the Mustangs won today, he'd most definitely be in front of a dozen sportscasters, and he'd bet good money they'd ask him about his love life.

They didn't win.

But by noon on Monday, he had evidence in his hand that people were buying tickets regardless, in record numbers. Logan McLaughlin had become the poster boy for the Dallas Mustangs ball club, and Myra had very specific ideas for how to capitalize on it.

Logan bit his tongue and picked up the phone to call Trinity.

Five

There was literally nothing about baseball that had matched Trinity's expectations. Case in point: when Logan had called her to ask if she'd go on a road trip with him, she'd actually thought he meant a *road trip*. Like the kind every single person on the planet except Logan would interpret as two people in a car driving somewhere.

Not what he'd meant.

Fortunately, jetting off to San Francisco for a few days to watch the Mustangs take on Oakland fit her need to not be at work on Monday. She might even call herself pathetically grateful to have a valid excuse for why she couldn't be at Fyra giving the nonexistent Formula-47 presentation.

Also, Logan had failed to mention that the Mustangs had a private plane for away games, which made the trip even more fun. The entire fuselage had been fitted with first-class-size seats, which made her feel even tinier in a cabin full of large men, but she reveled in the luxury.

Shortly after takeoff, the flight crew began circulating with drinks and food. Logan casually took Trinity's hand, lacing their fingers together. Strictly for show. She knew that. But it put a little tingle in her stomach that she secretly didn't hate.

She was looking forward to a lot more *tingle* in her future. After all, this trip was the perfect opportunity to take their relationship to the next level, both on camera and off.

"Tell me again," she murmured with a nod at the middle-aged man Logan had introduced her to earlier as the Mustangs' manager. "You're the general manager and that guy is the manager with no other title in front of it?"

"Right. It's a weird baseball thing. I never think twice about it." Logan's thumb brushed over her knuckle as he spoke and she wondered if he even realized he was doing it. "Gordon is the coach and I'm the CEO."

Prior to today, Logan had been almost deliberately affectionate, as if he was only paying attention to her because their on-camera relationship required it. She was trying not to ascribe any meaning to his seemingly subconscious touch other than the obvious—he was technically at work and probably focused on that.

Besides, they weren't a real couple. There didn't have to be meaning to anything he did. In public, everything was fake. She didn't have to dissect his moods or worry if he was thinking about ditching her. None of that mattered, which was what made it great.

"CEO, huh? So everyone reports to you and you could fire them all?"

He nodded with a shrug.

That was a job she was glad Cass had signed up for at Fyra. Trinity would hate having so many people looking to her for answers.

She scooched down in her seat. Wasn't that still the case with the marketing campaign for Formula-47? Skipping town on the wave of positive publicity didn't absolve the fact that a lot of people depended on her to hit a home run on this one.

And Logan had apparently invaded her consciousness to the point where she was making baseball analogies.

She'd noticed that around Logan, her muse was inspired. She'd gotten a double dose of inspiration from that scorching-hot round of kissing Saturday night, but the dozens of half-finished sketches hadn't moved her much closer to her goal. Something much more…*encompassing* than mere kissing might be the ticket, and she had a four-day trip ahead of her to prove her theory.

The next time she got naked with Logan, there would be a whole lot more happening than a conversation, and no one would be putting on clothes for quite a while. But she didn't want to clue him in that she had a stake in taking this very public flirtation behind closed doors.

When they got to the hotel, a slew of photographers waited outside the sliding glass doors. The limo Logan had chartered slid to a stop near the valet stand, but he didn't get out right away.

"By the way, I tipped off the local press that we were coming to this series. Together," he said. "As a couple. I hope that was okay."

"Brilliant." She'd wondered if this was the typical welcome a baseball team received in a host city. But it was the general manager and his girlfriend-slash-fiancée that they'd come to see. Nice. "Maybe we should think about hiring someone to follow us around with a camera. I like the organic reach of having unbiased third parties pick up the story, but it couldn't hurt to goose things a little."

"Got it covered. My publicist does, anyway," he amended as Trinity lifted her brows in question. "She's sending someone to all three games to take photos of us in my suite."

"We have a suite?" Like with a bed? Suddenly the prospect of sitting through three baseball games got a little more interesting. "You should have mentioned that way before now. Maybe we can take an adult nap during the middle part when nothing happens."

She waggled her brows to be sure he picked up on the double entendre.

His chuckle warmed her enormously. "It's not like a hotel suite. It's a skybox with seats for people to watch the action on the field, but with air-conditioning and a bar. I also invited several acquaintances to come hang out with us. It'll be a party."

Oh. That still sounded better than being outside in the sun while watching guys in uniforms hit a ball. "I shall be attentive and adoring in front of your friends. And the photographer."

Just that morning, a new article had made the rounds with damaging allegations about Fyra's animal testing practices. Cass had already involved their lawyer to see if they could sue. But anything Trinity could do to negate that bunch of BS would only help.

He climbed from the limo and helped her out, slipping an arm around her waist to guide her inside. The porter began pulling luggage from the limo's trunk as people surged forward, cameras poised to begin snapping money shots of the couple they'd come to photograph.

"Nice shoes," he murmured in her ear as flashes went off around them.

Yeah, she'd worn her six-inch Prada heels even though her ankles got puffy when she flew. The straps were cutting into her flesh and she'd lost feeling in her toes at least three hours ago. But she liked it when he could put his arm around her, too.

"You're welcome."

He grinned, and she promptly forgot about her ankles. Maybe she could talk him into an adult nap right this minute. Just to take the edge off. Her insides had never quite cooled after that second kiss Saturday night, and she'd be quite happy to pick up where they'd left off.

But then she distinctly heard him tell the hotel clerk *two rooms*. "What?"

He glanced at her. "One sec. I'm checking in."

"I realize that." She smiled at the clerk. "Excuse us for a moment, please."

The charter bus the rest of the team had ridden in from the airport picked that moment to unload. A wave of testosterone flowed through the doors, raising the noise level to a dull roar as the athletes, coaches and staff members sorted themselves out.

Dragging Logan to an uncrowded corner of the lobby was no small feat given both her precarious balance and his resemblance to an immovable mountain. But he came willingly, which she appreciated. She raised her brows. "Are you insane? We can't have separate rooms."

"We not only can, we are." He crossed his arms. "As soon as I get the keys, that is."

Aghast, she stared at him, but he looked perfectly serious. "After you went to the trouble to hire photographers, what are the odds they'll snap a picture of us going into separate rooms? Like a hundred and ten percent."

He scowled. "So? We can be a chaste couple waiting for marriage, can't we?"

His scowl deepened the harder she laughed. When she finally got herself under control, she gingerly dabbed at her eyelashes without fear thanks to Harper's waterproof, smudge-proof, morning after–proof mascara, all of which Trinity had personally tested.

"Did you actually look at the pictures from Saturday night?" She had. A lot. And twice she'd had to finish the job he'd started herself. Her vibrator hadn't ever gotten so much action. "They had ten times the reach that the ones from Friday did. The posed red carpet thing? Not for us. The spontaneous, hotter-than-hell, can't-wait-to-screw-each-other vibe is what our fans like. What they want to see."

His expression didn't change, and her panic level started an uphill climb. She needed him. Needed to get hot and heavy away from the camera. Inspiration was in short supply, and he was hogging it all.

"No. It's not happening. I've already made huge concessions—"

"Like what?" Hands on her hips, she forced her voice back down into a lower register before someone overheard them. She didn't mind if the photographers captured a public fight, but she did not want them to splash the cause of it across the web. "I'm the one constantly changing my clothes and—"

"One time you changed, and only because I forced you—"

"You so did not force me. I let you change my clothes because it suited me. Make no mistake, you don't control me."

"I don't want to, Trinity!" He apparently had no concept of volume, and several heads swiveled in their direction.

"Shh." She jerked her head at the press, who had

definitely clued in that something was afoot and started snapping away. Hopefully they'd get some good shots. "Act like you're mad all you want, but we can't afford any prying ears."

"I'm not acting," he growled. "I've already had phone calls about our impending engagement, despite your certainty that no one was going to ask about it. I don't like being put in that position. Nor do I want to be in the position of defending my personal choices regarding sleeping arrangements."

Gee whiz. His old-fashioned streak went a whole lot deeper than she'd credited. What a fun new challenge she'd stumbled onto here. Gaze narrowed, she swept him with a once-over designed to put a few thousand degrees of heat under his skin. "You must not be aware of what I have planned, then, if you think this is about sleeping."

Instantly, wariness and a fair amount of caution snapped across his expression. Who was throwing up shields now, hmm?

"Separate rooms," he said firmly.

"Fine."

She threw up her hands, but only to make it look like she still hated the idea, when actually, she'd realized it worked in her favor. It was a much juicier story if they had separate rooms but, oh, look, someone just caught them macking down in the hall outside one of them. And then they could both duck inside to take the super-hot kiss to its natural conclusion.

It was also in her best interests to ensure it was his room...so she could accidentally on purpose let someone photograph her sneaking away from it at dawn.

"Separate rooms. But you have to take me to dinner," she insisted. "Otherwise, we'll miss a golden opportunity to get more lens time."

He nodded with a smug smile. Probably because he thought he'd won. She let him think that. By the end of the night, he'd realize they'd both won.

One thing she could say for Logan, he did not cheap out when it came to putting up his fake girlfriend-slash-fiancée in a hotel.

Trinity took a long soak in the garden tub and used every ounce of the bubble bath the hotel had provided from their signature spa, strictly for market research purposes.

One hot-and-heavy sheet session with Logan could do the trick to get her muse back in the game full-time. But she was fully prepared to go all night with him if need be. Three or four orgasms fit into her schedule just fine, especially when Logan was the one delivering them. The man got her hotter than concrete in August.

In deference to her agenda, she selected a very simple white shift dress strewn with tiny colored flowers that covered her almost to the neck. It looked spectacular on her even though it didn't advertise any skin. To make up for the conservative dress, she put a pink stripe down the side of her hair and wore lace-up heels that crisscrossed her ankles a bajillion times. It would take both an enterprising and patient man to get these shoes off, and she shivered in anticipation of the foreplay that could be involved.

Logan knocked on her door.

She answered. His gaze dropped to her dress and lingered, hot appreciation blooming on his face. Score one for Trinity.

How had she missed that he liked her *that* much better in conventional clothes? He'd been so turned on by the simple jeans and T-shirt, but she'd mistakenly believed that had been a result of him being the one to put them on her.

"I expected to have to redress you," he threw out casually, but she did not miss the undercurrent of disappointment. He not only liked her in conservative clothes, he liked picking them out. Road trips made for interesting fonts of information, that was for sure.

"I was feeling generous."

"Noted. I will return the favor by escorting you to a nice dinner."

Where she would be charming and pretend that dinner was the only photo op of the night.

As predicted, a few photographers were still hanging around in the lobby, and she and Logan dutifully stopped before continuing on to the restaurant, allowing pictures. It didn't matter that the photos were staged, because they would all pale in comparison to the ones later on tonight, anyway. These chaste pictures got them nowhere.

Dinner was surprisingly normal. And nice. Logan exhibited incredible patience as Trinity peppered him with baseball questions that he must have found tedious. But she liked listening to him talk about his passion, and baseball was clearly it. He talked with his hands, smiled, laughed. If she didn't know better, she'd think they were actually dating.

No. Slipping into a fantasy about this whole thing being real was the surest path to problems.

"Walk me to my room?" she asked casually after noting several photographers had drifted away. Only the most tenacious had hung on, which meant they would likely be the most interested in being thrown a bone.

"Sure." Logan laced his fingers with hers in what had become a very common move for him. She liked it, but that was a deep, dark secret she'd never spill.

Was this what normal couples did, how they acted with each other? Was that why so many people did the relationship deal despite the surety of things going south? If nothing else, participating in a fake relationship gave her an inkling why Cass, Alex and Harper had all jumped on the marriage bandwagon.

But none of her friends were broken. Obviously. Just because real relationships had happened for them didn't mean it would for Trinity. That's why this one was so great—it would end before anyone got attached.

Of course, they hadn't exactly established an expiration date, but he could announce one any second. Letting go of Logan suddenly felt like the very last thing she'd be okay with, and her throat tightened along with her hand.

He squeezed hers back and oh, God, she didn't want to let him go. Not tonight.

They stepped out of the elevator on her floor without any reporters following them, and she didn't care. None of this was about the press or sales. He was a man and she was a woman and she needed him. For a lot of things, some she didn't even want to articulate to herself, let alone to him.

Logan must have sensed her distress, because he lifted her hand to his lips and kissed two knuckles as they arrived at her door. "What's wrong? You're shaking."

"Nothing." *Blow it off.* Not letting a man see her weaknesses was so ingrained, she did it automatically. "Just thinking about our missed opportunity to get photographed kissing downstairs."

"We have the next three days. We'll have plenty of opportunities."

She couldn't let him leave. Desperately, she shook her head and smiled, easily falling into seduce-and-conquer mode. Because that's what she knew how to do. "Maybe we should practice."

He laughed. "Kissing? You saw the pictures from Saturday. I don't think lack of practice is our problem."

"No, it's not," she murmured. "Our problem is that we always stop."

A glint popped into his gaze that she couldn't read. But he wasn't walking away. "We stop because we're in public and our agreement doesn't extend to making X-rated films."

But not because he *wanted* to stop. She pounced on that small distinction and held up her card key, then deliberately dragged it down his torso until she hit his belt. "So don't stop."

If he didn't, it would be her one chance to pretend Logan could be hers for real. Just for one night.

The little white dress Trinity wore had been killing him since he'd first glimpsed her in it. All Logan could think about during dinner was putting his hands under it to see if she had on virginal white underwear or had gone full-bore bad girl with a racy thong, maybe in red.

Either one would work.

The mystery could be solved very easily. All he had to do was sweep her into his arms, open the door and lay her out on the hotel bed.

He didn't. There were rules in place. For a reason.

"Are you inviting me into your room?" His voice had dropped, going raw with need that he couldn't control if he tried. So he wasn't trying. "Because that would be a no-no. We're only a couple in public. A fake couple."

"Oh, right. We're still worried about your rule book." She didn't sound worried. She sounded like she was about to rip all of his rules to shreds. And maybe some of his sanity, too. "If it would make you feel better, we could leave the door open."

A technicality. It had potential. If they left the door open, they'd theoretically still be a couple. It was only behind closed doors that he'd established any sort of parameters.

"That doesn't make it real," he cautioned, and he was pretty sure she realized he was talking to himself more than her.

Kissing in public was one thing, but to take it behind closed doors meant he had to admit his fierce attraction to Trinity went far deeper than it should. She wasn't the right woman for him.

Her laugh ripped through his groin, hardening his shaft to the point of pain.

"For the love of all that's holy, Logan. Please tell me what about the sizzling-hot thing between us isn't real?"

She had a point, one he wished he didn't like so much. Real was relative.

They had a real attraction. A real interest in getting each other naked. The only fake part was how it had started. And how it would end. He'd always defined a real relationship as one with potential to be permanent, but again, perspective.

"What are you saying, that we'd become a real couple?" he asked.

What did that even mean? How would they manage the logistics of that?

"Sweetie, you're thinking about all of this way too hard." She took his hand and flipped it over, exposing his palm, where she laid her room key as some kind of offering. Or challenge. "We don't need rules or definitions. That's how things get all messed up. All we need is to know that once we step through that door, we're both going to have a lot of orgasms. Together."

Something akin to relief rushed through his body along with a very strong lick of lust that put every nerve on high alert. She was doing her best to make this all about sex. Which was working. What did it matter whether she was a woman he could marry or not? That wasn't on the table, for either of them. Why was he even struggling with this?

She closed his fingers around her room key. "This is your show, Logan. If you want to play this as a publicity angle, I'm all for it. Think about how much sizzle photographs of us will have if we're actually burning up the sheets. It's a no-brainer."

The key to everything was literally in his hand. She'd given him the choice—wisely—because then he couldn't say he hadn't made it. "You're just going to keep throwing out my rules until I give in, aren't you?"

Wickedness laced her smile. "I'm pretty sure I already have. Oh, wait. I forgot rule number one. Logan McLaughlin, I dare you to take what you want. Let me fulfill every last fantasy you've ever had but were too busy being nice to indulge in."

That was the sexiest thing a woman had ever said to him.

"Every one?" he murmured. She didn't move, but thick, dense awareness rolled between them like fog with teeth, weighting his words. "I'm afraid even you couldn't keep up with my vivid imagination. It's been in high gear pretty much since the moment you told me you had a tongue piercing."

"Try me."

The chemistry that had been building since day one exploded inside him, and he pressed her up against the door before he could think. Not thinking worked for him. She'd given him permission to feel and he planned to.

Mouth on hers, he angled her head in a fiery kiss that flowed through him, hot, molten. When she added her tongue, he sucked it in greedily. Sensation cleaved across his flesh as she worked that steel bar.

He had so many fantasies about that thing. Where to start?

Her lush little body didn't fit against his the way he wanted, so he wedged a hand under her thigh and boosted her higher against the door until his raging erection slid into the valley between her thighs.

She moaned in a register that drove him insane. When she felt pleasure, she let him know. That was powerful, and it burst open something inside him. He wanted more of that, more of her under his mouth, more of her crying out his name.

But they were still in the hall. Because he hadn't yet committed.

It was time to take this behind closed doors.

Scrabbling with the plastic in his hand, he somehow got it into the slot without letting go of her. The door swung open, and just so there was no opportunity for either of them to throw down another roadblock, he picked her up to carry her across the threshold. It was symbolic, maybe more for him than her, but her feminine sigh unfolded something inside him as he kicked the door shut.

When he laid her out on the bed, he meant to immediately dive back into the kiss he'd had to cut short with the room entrance logistics. But he paused for a half second to drink her in, because she was a stunning sight, lounging there on the bedspread wearing that simple white dress. She'd put it on for no other reason than because she wanted to please him.

She had. She did. Constantly, even when they were crossing swords. A lot of times, he didn't even care if he won the battle because the act of fighting it turned him on. It should bother him. How messed up was that? But everything about her turned him on, and he was done resisting it.

But before he could get started on the million or so fantasies he'd lined up in his mind, she rolled to her knees and reached for his belt buckle, drawing him closer as she peered up through her lashes. "I can't wait to taste you."

His shaft grew impossibly harder, and it took a supreme amount of will to gather his faculties enough to still her hands. She'd already gotten his belt unbuckled and had started to pull it from its mooring.

"No," he said hoarsely. "That's not what I want."

Obviously his meaning did not compute, because she cocked a brow and broke free of his hold to yank the belt completely off. "In case I'm not being clear, I'm going down on you. Right now."

"I wasn't confused."

His eyelids shuttered closed as she trailed her fingers across his erection. Her touch through his clothes felt like liquid fire, and he nearly came at the thought of her mouth on his flesh. The real thing would probably be the death of him, but he wasn't going to find out. Not at this moment, anyway.

What she wanted was to stay in control. She wasn't going to get her wish.

The sound of his zipper sliding open put a little more urgency in that thought. Encircling her wrists, he drew her quick fingers away from his body. "Stop, Trinity. As good as I'm sure that would be, that's not what I fantasize about."

Bewilderment marred her face. "Really? Not ever?"

He groaned. "Of course I've thought about it. I'm not the Goody Two-shoes you seem to think I am. But neither am I a selfish ass who only thinks about how great it would be to have a woman go down on me."

"You'd be in a small minority of one," she muttered. "I have to ask. What in the world do you fantasize about then?"

Now they were talking. He eased her backward on the bed, still holding her wrists, until they hit the bedspread. Nuzzling her neck, he held her hands captive as he lightly sucked on her skin, diabolically pleased with the gasp that burst from her throat.

"I fantasize about being the man you moan for," he murmured against her skin. "The one who makes you come so many times, you don't remember what it's like to be with anyone else. I'm guessing you've had a lot of sex in your life, Trinity. But you've never been with me before, and I guarantee you this will be nothing like any of those times."

"So it's a competition thing?"

That was so not it. But neither did he know how to be someone other than who he was. He liked to feel something inside when he made love to a woman. A connection. His gut told him the surest way to get that with Trinity was to not let her do things the way she always did.

"Is it so difficult to believe that I want to give you a unique experience?"

"When it comes down to a choice between me pleasuring you or the other way around, yeah." The disbelief in her voice sliced through him, and it scored a place inside he wouldn't have said she could reach.

As many times as she'd surely gotten naked with a

man, had she never had *one* who cared about her pleasure above his own?

That was not okay.

He lifted his head and released her wrists at the same time in favor of threading her inky hair through his fingers. The thumb he brushed across her cheek put a note of tenderness in the moment that he hadn't intended... but there it was. "So then I have to ask. What do *you* fantasize about?"

Something akin to shock zipped across her expression, but she covered it almost immediately. "Making a man come with my mouth."

He grinned. "How many times have you said that? You must practice in the mirror, because it was impressive how you spit it out without having to think about it. Now give me the real answer. Otherwise, I'm going to have to work my way through all the things I can think of until I figure it out for myself."

"Maybe that's what I want," she said flippantly. "Maybe that's what I was after all along."

Yeah, he didn't think so. The wild uncertainty in her gaze told a different story, one that he should be ashamed he liked so much. But Trinity unsettled and off-kilter might be the sexiest she'd been yet. That was a state he could get into a whole hell of lot more.

He wanted her naked and writhing under him as he gave her orgasm after orgasm until she was so spent, she forgot all about her need for control.

And she was going to like it.

Six

Trinity swallowed as Logan's big palms engulfed her face. The kiss he laid on her lips had far too much sweetness in it. Like he wanted this thing between them to be real as much as she did.

I want to see the real you.

The request—demand—he'd made when he'd changed her clothes suddenly took on new meaning. Maybe she'd let him see her for reasons she hadn't fully admitted to herself. Her chest quivered with some nameless, unfathomable emotions. Which was not supposed to be the deal.

She'd given him permission to make this about nothing more than sex. Tried to stick to that herself. She'd practically had his zipper down and her hands on his rock-hard shaft, which she wanted to see with her own two eyes but hadn't yet, because he'd shifted gears so hard in the other direction, she still didn't know what had happened.

He'd *stopped* her from giving him the first of many climaxes.

What was he trying to do to her?

"I've been wondering," he murmured, "about what you have on under that dress."

"I've been wondering how long it would take you to find out," she shot back. Except the sassy note she'd tried to slip into her tone hadn't come out like she'd wanted.

Instead, it had sounded wistful.

With a wicked smile that shouldn't have tripped so many alarms in her head, he put his hands on her knees to situate her the way he seemed to want: shoes on the ground, bottom nearly to the edge of the bed, thighs open wide. He knelt between her legs and slid both palms along her skin, his rough hands thrilling her as he gathered the fabric in a slow reveal that hitched her lungs.

The ivy tattoo appeared. He settled his mouth on the first green leaf and dragged his tongue across it. Gasping, she bowed off the bed and levered herself up on her elbows, because she didn't want to miss anything.

The sight of his beautiful mouth on her thigh did it for her like nothing else.

"More where that came from," he murmured.

He licked her tattoo clear up to her panties, shoving back her dress and fingering the fabric of her white thong. "I'm going to take this off."

"You don't have to check in with me," she informed him breathlessly. Now that he'd so thoroughly turned the tables, she couldn't get air into her lungs. She ached for him to touch her intimately, and she wanted it now. "Really, I'm game for whatever you have in mind."

He glanced up, his expression hooded and implacable. "It would be best if you'd clue in right up front that I do things my own way. Therefore, I will be telling you what I'm doing to you as I do it. For example, I'm about to put my tongue between your legs."

The promise raked heat through her core. Logan McLaughlin had a dirty mouth, and she was a huge fan of it.

Hooking his fingers at the waistband of her thong, he slid it off and tossed it over his shoulder. His gaze went hot as he looked his fill at her uncovered sex. No one had ever done anything like that before. Sure, she'd had men go down on her, but usually in the dark, and most of the time it had a mechanical, scripted vibe as if there was some unwritten rule that she had to get off before her partner got his turn. In short, not very romantic.

This…was.

Logan had already eliminated his pleasure from this equation, and it was as unsettling as it was exciting. It was easy to take what she wanted from a man after he'd done the same to her, but she had no idea how to accept pleasure freely given.

"Trinity," he murmured, and her name floated across her skin like a prayer. "You're so gorgeously made. I want to taste all of you at once. I hardly know where to start."

She fought the urge to say something outrageous, to deflect, to ease her discomfort. She didn't know how to deal with a man who wasn't letting her run the show. He took away her dilemma by easing his thumbs up her thighs until he hit her slick center, where he went on an exploring mission that instantly lit her up.

Eventually, he replaced his thumbs with his lips.

Her core flooded with heat, and she gasped as he draped one of her knees over his shoulder, moving closer to her, increasing the pressure, the hot, wet sensation that had her crying out as she soared toward the ceiling. His tongue—it felt like it was everywhere at once, thanks to the sheer power of suggestion.

His big, solid hands held her in place as her hips bucked against his mouth. He welcomed it, going deeper, harder, faster until her skin incinerated under his onslaught and she came with his name on her lips.

"Again," he murmured, his lips grazing her core as he spoke. "Don't hold back. I want to watch you."

He fingered her pulsing channel, catching the faint echoes of her orgasm and whipping her into a frenzy instantly. Her back lifted from the bed as he shot sparks through her entire body, shoving her over the cliff a second time. She crashed into the release with something akin to shock, letting it play out in a way she never had before. In a way she'd never been able to before.

Bleary eyed, she stared up at him as he covered her, dipping his head to take her mouth, sharing the earthy taste of herself on his tongue. It was as arousing as it was intimate.

Good sex stems from intimacy. It wasn't just a throwaway comment he'd made. The man meant what he said. Always. Instead of enticing the all-American boy to take a walk on the wild side, he'd yanked her firmly over to his side. But she had no time to reflect on the irony of that as he shifted her to her stomach so he could unzip her dress.

This time, he offered no explanation as he stripped her of her dress and bra. When she was naked, he laid her back on the pillow and picked up one foot. He took one look at the tangled mess of strings and grinned. Wickedly.

"Is this some kind of Mensa test?" He yanked on one

firmly tangled string. "Let's see if the good ole Texas boy is smart enough to figure out how to get this off."

"Maybe." She shrugged and matched his smile. "Maybe it's an opportunity to prove how badly you want it."

"Sweetheart, you underestimate me." With that, he dropped her shoe to the bed. "I can do all sorts of things to you without taking them off, which I don't mind one bit, and you're the one who has to wear them during, so…we'll have a discussion later about our individual intellects."

With that, he rolled from the bed and did the most provocative striptease she'd ever seen in her life. First he slipped all his shirt's buttons from their moorings and inch by inch revealed the torso she'd felt plenty of times but was only now getting her first glimpse of.

There might have been drooling.

Then he took off his shirt, first from one broad shoulder, then the other, and the final product dried up her mouth to the point where drooling was definitely not in her future, along with not breathing. The man was magnificent, hard, sinewy, clearly not an executive who spent a lot of time behind a desk. Or wearing a shirt. He had a tan line where the sleeves of his many and varied T-shirts hit his biceps, but he must do something outside with his chest bared because it was deliciously sun kissed, highlighting what blew past a six-pack into uncharted territory.

She'd have to count the indentions across his abs. With her tongue.

The prospect unleashed a shiver. He undid his pants and let them drop to the floor along with whatever underwear he might have had on, and then she was really glad she was already lying down, because holy hell.

Powerful thighs. Thick erection. Too much to take in. No words.

But she didn't need any as he retrieved a handful of condoms from his pants pocket, which she scarcely had time to register. Though they'd circle back to the fact that he'd had condoms *in his pocket* the entire time.

And then there was no more thinking as he gathered her up and settled her into the grooves of his body. The hard, brutal planes of his physique had no give, and she thrilled at the feel of it against her bare skin.

He tipped up her head with both hands and she fell into the kiss, instantly drowning in Logan. Their legs entwined and his muscular thigh came up between hers, seeking her sweet spot…and finding it, rubbing hard at her still-sensitive bits until gray blurred her vision and a gasp tore from her throat.

Her skin heated so quickly she feared she might burn to ash. His hot hands spanned her waist, rolling her to her back. Taking one nipple in his talented mouth, he nipped and sucked until her back arched, and she had enough brain cells to realize he was doing exactly as he'd promised—pleasuring her with no thought to himself. He'd already made her come twice and seemed in no rush to stop.

What do you fantasize about?

She'd done precious little of that in her life. Her creativity was usually drained by the end of the day, and by the time she got naked with a man, it was never about what she wanted.

Why was it never about what she wanted?

Logan's teeth hit a spot on her nipple that barreled through her like a freight train, and she cried out.

"I love it when you do that," he murmured. "It's like an aphrodisiac."

Since aphrodisiac should be his middle name, she liked it, too. "Maybe you should see what switching to the other side gets you."

He chuckled and did exactly that, dragging his tongue across the valley between her breasts as he went, and then sucked her other nipple into his hot mouth. But he coupled that with a very well-placed finger between her legs, and the dual sensations spun her off into oblivion again. Breathless, she clenched her way through another spectacular orgasm that encompassed her whole body.

Logan had a condom rolled on and was poised at her entrance, pushing inside before her vision cleared. Mewling sounds tore from her throat as the pressure built, and it was so good, so unbelievable on the heels of a release. He grabbed one stiletto and tugged her knee nearly to her shoulder as he widened her.

"Relax," he murmured. "I'm…big."

Yeah, she'd noted that for herself. "You say that like I should be disappointed. That's usually on the pro side of a girl's checklist."

Oh, yes, he *was* big. Her whole body went liquid as the exquisite feel of his length slid along her sensitized flesh.

But not too big. Perfect. Especially after he'd primed her to the point where she was so swollen and wet that he slid in easily. And she didn't miss that he'd done so. Even in this, he was thinking about her pleasure instead of taking his own.

When he'd buried himself inside completely, he sucked in a breath and froze, bliss stealing across his features. "You feel so amazing."

How was he forming coherent sentences? Her own body had wheeled off into the stratosphere, greedily sucking in all the new sensations as he began to move, circling his hips as he thrust. She couldn't have stopped the moans pouring from her throat at gunpoint and she didn't want to. He murmured his encouragement with well-placed phrases as they came together again and again.

The best was when he wrapped her leg around his waist and let go of her stiletto in favor of cupping her jaw. But he didn't kiss her, just watched her as he plunged deep inside, his eyes dark and focused. Fingers tangled in his hair, she couldn't look away, even when his face tightened and turned tender with release. It was so powerful to witness such a strong man showing his vulnerability that she nearly came apart inside.

When was the last time she'd done it missionary style? It was her least favorite position—or at least it had been until Logan.

He made it exquisite, an experience. Not just sex, but pleasure combined with connection, both beautiful and precious.

This was what she fantasized about. A man who would be the same in bed or out, day in and day out. Still there in the morning. Strong, capable. Honest. One who cared about her over his own selfish needs.

She fantasized about being loved.

And she'd spent the last few years of her life systematically ensuring she'd never have to think about the fact that she didn't have that, wasn't capable of having that.

Which meant she had to shove that particular fantasy back into the deep. Where it belonged.

The pictures from outside Trinity's door the night before shot their fake relationship into the stratosphere.

Apparently some of the photographers from the lobby had followed them after all.

Logan downed the first of what would likely be many cups of coffee that morning as he ate breakfast in the small dining room of the hotel restaurant and reread the email from Myra crowing about his brilliant strategy to be photographed kissing Trinity outside her hotel room.

If you could call it that. Strategy hadn't been forefront in his mind. And it was hard to label it something as innocuous as a kiss.

The scene was almost pornographic, raw and sensual, and the photographer had timed it perfectly to show Trinity's card key clutched in his fingers as he searched blindly for the slot without even lifting his mouth from hers. The urgency burned visibly between them.

He almost couldn't look at the picture. It was too much truth, too intimate. Had Trinity known a photographer had followed them upstairs? Was that the only reason she'd given him the green light?

Last night had been real—to him, anyway. As real as the ache in his elbow from the vigorous activity, which had caused his old injury to flare up. And it didn't sit well that something so personal had been captured and then turned into a marketing gimmick by his and Trinity's respective publicists.

But that's what they'd been doing all along. Why was this picture different? He didn't like the answer. Or the kick to his stomach as he glanced up to see Trinity breeze into the restaurant and take a seat at his table without so much as a hello.

God, she was gorgeous. Even with an inch-wide green stripe running down the nonshaved side of her hair. He was almost accustomed to the heavy hand she used to apply her cosmetics, and honestly, it was part of the overt style that bled from her pores. She wore a flowy, hair-stripe-matching grass-green dress that covered her to her calves and tied up around her neck. She looked so sizzling hot that he had his suit jacket unbuttoned before he realized he'd been about to take it off so he could cover her up with it.

Moron. She'd shredded his brain cells last night.

It was a very respectable dress. It was what was under the dress that got him, and he didn't just mean the body. Trinity was fierce on the outside, but when he'd gotten her behind closed doors, she'd melted into his arms, becoming so sweet and impassioned he could hardly fathom it.

That had been a huge surprise. And all he wanted to do this morning was pull her into his lap and stick his nose into that juncture of her neck and shoulder, where it most smelled like her. Then he'd start peeling back her outrageous shell again.

"Lara called me already," Trinity said as she smiled at the waitress and ordered coffee. "My publicist. She's thrilled with the traffic on our website. I have a couple of calls in to Alex to get some prelim sales numbers now that it's close enough to the end of the month to have the data."

"Good morning to you, too," he said and almost didn't choke on it.

Trinity shot him a look. "Get up on the wrong side of the bed? Or maybe in the wrong bed entirely? I told you to stay. You were the one who insisted on propriety and left."

Because he'd had to. Sleeping in the same bed with her put a stamp of permanence on this association that he couldn't afford. Not as far as the outside world was concerned; it was already too late for that. But in his mind. They were a real couple now, for better or worse, and he wasn't sorry they'd taken things to the next level. But it was *temporarily* real.

He couldn't forget that. Sleeping with her, wrapped up in each other all night long, would be a mistake.

Instead of letting the unsettled restlessness in his chest take over his mood, he lifted her hand from the table and kissed her palm. "My publicist is happy with the results as well. Act like you're enjoying yourself. There's a slew of photographers across the way."

She peered in the direction of his subtle head jerk from the corner of her eye to where a crowd of people lined the lobby, visible over the low wall separating the restaurant from the rest of the ground floor. "They're here early. And I don't have to act like I'm having fun with you. I just do."

Really? He eyed her. "You're in Oakland, California, at a hotel eating crappy breakfast food, and I'm about to make you watch a baseball game that you don't want to sit through. You should have higher standards."

Her smile heated him so fast, his vision grayed. "It's what will happen after the game that's keeping my spirits up."

And now he was thinking about that, too. He'd been trying not to, because they hadn't really established any morning-after rules, like how frequently they'd take their relationship behind closed doors. Given that they'd be doing deliberate on-camera work today as well, maybe she'd want a break. What did he know about what went on in her head?

"The endless interviews and postgame strategy sessions?" he commented. "Yeah, that'll be a blast for you."

She'd agreed to do the whole nine yards' worth of

press junkets in hopes of getting some extra exposure, which had seemed necessary at the time but now felt excessive given that they were already burning up the internet with their presex activities in the hall.

"You're so sweet to worry about me." Her hand was still in his, and she thumbed his knuckle almost affectionately. "But I can amuse myself. All I have to do is think about how much it'll be killing you to stand next to me, knowing that I'm completely naked under this dress."

Hot coffee scalded his throat as he choked on it.

Clearly nowhere nearly as concerned as she should be—since his inability to breathe or swallow was her fault—she arched a brow. "Are you okay?"

"What do you think?" he growled. "Are you really commando? Like, one hundred percent?"

She nodded with a sly smile. "And I plan to sit really close to you during the game. Maybe there will be a table that might cover a wandering hand or two?"

That dress took on a whole new definition of shock value—and now he definitely wanted to cover her up. With his naked body.

Going commando under a simple dress should definitely be a morning-after rule. He just couldn't decide if the rule should state *never* or *always*.

Trinity chatted some more about strategy and photo ops while drinking her coffee and refusing to eat anything, a female tendency he could never understand. The team had already left for the stadium so they could get started on their pregame rituals. Ballplayers were a superstitious lot, and you couldn't pry their customs from their cold, dead fingers. They always ate at the ballpark, mostly so Gordon could watch the players like a hawk, but also because hotel food sucked.

Normally, he'd be with them, angsting alongside the coaches. But instead of doing his job, Logan was still at the hotel, listening to his fake girlfriend–slash–real lover talk about how great it was that this partnership was paying off.

"Fyra was featured in a cosmetic review on *Allure's* website," she gushed. "And it was so positive that our northeast distribution warehouse is out of stock of Bahama Sunset eye shadow and the mascara they mentioned. They panned us last time, claiming the products they tried were overpriced. Like anyone cares about value when it comes to whether your mascara clumps or not."

"Uh-huh." Her lips moved constantly and he couldn't help but think about how quiet she got when it counted. When talking wasn't necessary because they were communicating perfectly with their bodies.

He wasn't done with his fantasies, that was for sure. And for the first time in his life, he resented the fact that he couldn't just watch a baseball game with a gorgeous woman and then take her back to his room for some postgame activities. Maybe he could cut things shorter than normal. He was already making concessions by not being on the field at this moment.

"We'll leave in about an hour," he told her as they left the restaurant after breakfast.

"Oh. Isn't the game at one o'clock?"

He hid a smile. "Yeah, but the team usually gets there about six hours early. I'm cutting you a break since it's your first time."

She hit the lobby an hour later, exactly on time. The day was perfect for baseball—cloudy with a slight breeze off the bay, which put the temperature near sixty degrees. Logan loved this area, especially in the sum-

mer, when it routinely reached 110 in their home stadium in Texas. Trinity shivered as they stepped outside
the glass doors to the valet stand.

Without hesitation, he stripped off his jacket and
draped it around her shoulders. Gratefully, she smiled
and slipped her arms into the sleeves. He didn't feel
guilty at all about getting extra clothes on her and bit
his tongue instead of asking if she owned a sweater.

He was pretty sure he already knew the answer to
that.

Somehow he resisted putting his hands on her during
the limo ride to the field. The stadium sat overlooking the
bay with a great view of the Oakland bridge. Across the
bay, San Francisco gleamed in the low light of the morning, and he was extraordinarily glad they didn't have
to venture to that side of the bridge. The traffic in the
Bay Area rivaled Dallas, and he was not a fan of sitting
in the car for hours.

Of course, he'd never done it with Trinity. That might
make a long commute worth it.

The stadium was less grand than some others, but
he got a rush walking through the gates regardless. The
smell of popcorn lingered in the air, something almost
all stadiums had in common, even the open-air ones.
He'd never lost the sense of being on sacred ground, and
no matter what time it was, he could hear the thunk of
the ball against his glove, the shush as it sailed through
the air, the roar of the crowd in his head. God, he could
still feel the energy even though it had been nine years
since the last time he'd pitched here.

Some days it felt like his life had ended when his
career had.

Trinity slipped her hand into his, squeezing it. More
strategy? If she'd noticed he'd slipped into a funk, she

didn't say anything, but the timing couldn't be a coincidence. She'd somehow tuned in to him and he didn't hate it, no matter how weird it felt to be here with a woman, especially one wearing his suit jacket. Weird, but nice.

Trinity oohed and ahhed over the skybox he'd borrowed from a friend. He tried to see it through the eyes of someone who'd never been in one before, but he'd grown up in the box his dad owned, often hanging out for hours on random Saturdays during the season.

It was odd to be above the field when his team was on it. The players were warming up, and he automatically assessed each one.

Trinity's unique feminine scent hit him a moment before the woman did. She joined him at the glass overlooking the field. "Are you okay? You seem distant."

He shrugged, mystified how she could do that when he hadn't clued in on her moods to the same degree. "I'm an in-the-trenches guy. It's very unusual for me to watch my team play from this vantage point."

"Why are you here, then?"

It was a valid question. No one else was here yet. The party wouldn't start for a couple of hours, closer to game time. And there certainly weren't any photographers around. "I don't know."

He literally had no idea how to integrate a woman—fake, real or otherwise—into the rest of his life. Sure, he'd dated a few women here and there since buying the Mustangs. But they'd never been serious enough relationships to bring the lady to a game.

Which of course begged the question—how serious was this one?

There might have been a hundred other things he

could have taken his fake girlfriend to besides an away game, where they'd be stuck together for three more days until they went home late Thursday night. Yet he'd pounced on Myra's suggestion. Why, because he'd wanted to see how Trinity fit in here?

Trinity cocked her head, contemplating him. "If you're normally down on the field, the only conclusion I can draw is that you're here for me."

He made the mistake of meeting her ice-blue eyes, which had gained a great deal of warmth as she watched him.

"I am." No point in lying about it. "I didn't want you to be alone. This is a big stadium, and you don't know anything about baseball."

Okay, that part might not have been the whole truth. But he wasn't sure what was.

She laughed. "I'm a big girl, Logan. I can find things to do no matter where I am. But since you've made such an excellent point, tell me about baseball."

Eyeing the green dress and sandals she wore, he crossed his arms. "Really? Like all of it?"

"Sure." She uncrossed his arms for him without his permission and guided him to the long leather couch on the front row of the seating in the box. "We have time, right?"

He settled onto the cushion next to her, but only because he'd just realized the benefits of having this suite to themselves with no danger of her undergarments going missing.

The protective one-way film on the glass suddenly seemed like genius on the part of the stadium planners. No one could see in. No one could enter the suite without the lock code, and all the people who were privy to it wouldn't arrive for quite some time.

He had a temporary pass to have real sex with his fake girlfriend. That was the only thing he should—could—focus on right now. It was all they had between them that was real. All he could allow to be real.

Things had just gotten a hell of a lot more interesting.

Seven

"We have a couple of hours," Logan told her and picked up Trinity's hand to raise it to his lips, nibbling on her fingertips because he wanted to and he could. "What do you want to know about baseball?"

"I want to know everything."

Her voice had dropped into that register that somehow plugged straight into his groin, lighting it up. She pulled her hand from his grasp deliberately, with a little tsk. Without taking her eyes off him, she hiked up her skirt to flash him a very quick peek at her naked sex and levered one gorgeous leg over his lap, settling herself astride him.

Oh, God, yes.

Her heat ravaged his instant erection, burning him thoroughly even through his clothes. She leaned forward, rolling her hips to increase the contact between their bodies, and nuzzled his ear as she murmured, "Tell me what baseball means to you."

His pulse went into a free fall.

"Baseball is like breathing," he said hoarsely as her fingers went to work on his buttons.

He should stop her for... some reason. Because she was taking control. That was a bad thing. But he couldn't find any fault in the way she worked her hips against his length, and he groaned as she laved at his exposed collarbone.

"Breathing?" she prompted, tonguing her way up his throat.

He liked her out of control, when he was the one calling the shots. But his head tipped back easily as she cupped his jaw to move him into a position she liked better, and he was pretty sure he wasn't going to stop her. "I don't have to remind myself how much I enjoy the way my lungs function. They just do. I step on the mound and my body automatically cues up into the right stance to throw."

"What else?" She opened his shirt, her clever hands sliding down his torso to explore every inch of it, and her touch enflamed him. His thoughts fragmented as he fell into a sensuous haze, and words just spilled out from somewhere inside.

"My mind turns the ball over and over, examining it, hearing the way it sounds in the air. In my peripheral vision, I'm checking out first base to see if the guy has a little too much of a leadoff. The sun is usually high in the sky and I have to adjust my cap. But that guy at bat? He's not getting a piece of my arm."

"Logan, that's beautiful," she murmured and cupped his face with her hot hands, laying a kiss on his lips that he felt deep inside. When she pulled back, her eyes glowed with something he couldn't name, an appreciation, maybe, for what he'd shared without really meaning to. "You're a pitcher."

It wasn't a question, but he nodded as his throat worked, and he couldn't swallow all at once. None of that should have come so automatically, and she'd clued in that it was significant. Somehow. He'd never told her that he'd played professionally. That it still killed him on a regular basis that he wasn't down on the field at this moment warming up.

Sometimes being in the dugout with the team let him pretend for a few moments that he would actually don a uniform. Up here in a box? No way to maintain that illusion.

So here he was perpetuating another one. With Trinity.

When had he become so dependent on fantasy?

And how had she figured that out about him?

Before he could gather his scattered wits, she kissed him again, but this time, it had far more intent. Her mouth slanted against his, growing more heated and deliberate. Her tongue wound against his, seeking more, going deeper, and he helplessly fell into her, because he didn't care if it was supposed to be fake.

He wanted this woman as bare to him as he'd just been to her.

The tangle of their bodies pressed intimately together and her hips circled harder, faster against him. He reacted instantly, his insides turning molten until he couldn't feel his bones any longer. *Closer.* He needed her, ached to be inside her, and put his hands on her waist to hold her in place as he ground into her core, his shaft so hard between them it was a wonder he didn't bruise her tender flesh.

"Logan," she murmured. "Let me pleasure you."

And then she easily broke his hold, dropping to the ground between his legs. Her lithe hands went to work on his belt buckle, and before he could think of a reason to stop her, she yanked down his zipper, burrowing into his clothes to hit bare flesh.

He sucked in a breath as she peered up at him and simultaneously cupped him in her hot hands, running his tip along the line of her lips. He jerked involuntarily as sensation rocketed up his length.

The raw mood she'd uncovered twined with the physical reaction, making everything feel ten times more powerful.

"You're so beautiful," she crooned. "I'm going to take care of you. Let me show you how good this tongue piercing can make you feel."

So much blood rushed south he didn't understand how his heart could still be beating, but his pulse thundered in his ears, so things must still be in working order.

And then the entire world slid sideways as she dragged her tongue up his length. The bite of the steel coupled with her hot, rough lick nearly separated his bones from his skin. Then she sucked him fully into her mouth and he was lost to the dual sensations of cold and heat.

The emotional vortex inside him heightened everything.

Higher and higher she spun him. It was so good that his hips bucked automatically, shoving him deeper into her mouth, but she took him, *all of him*, and it felt unbelievable. So amazing that he couldn't hold back, couldn't stop the flood of Trinity through his blood, and his thighs tensed with the effort it took to simply keep breathing.

The release pounded through his entire body, ripping

a cry from his throat that was one hundred percent primal, and it was easily the hardest he'd ever come in his life. She finished him off expertly and he fell back on the couch, nerveless and so spent he couldn't feel his toes.

But the sated serenity that stole over him was so very right.

The sight of her on her knees before him, with her lips wrapped around him, had burned into his mind indelibly. She tucked him away and disappeared for a moment, then came back to settle into his side on the couch, lifting his arm so she could snuggle against his chest with his arm around her.

It was so nice, his eyes closed automatically as he soaked in the feel of her warm body bleeding through his. "You know I won't ever think about pitching again without thinking of your tongue piercing, right?"

She laughed, her fingers toying with one of the buttons hanging from his shirt. "I wanted to give you a unique experience. Since you did that for me. Last night."

The information she'd just shared filtered through his poor, beleaguered brain. "You mean I was successful?"

Of course, their conversation had been extremely limited last night because their mouths had been on each other, not talking.

Her smile was a little misty. "Let's just say I have a lot of selfish men in my past and I'm not sorry they're in my rearview mirror. Plus, I'm looking forward to how you're going to repay me for that."

"Yeah?" he growled. "Lucky for you I've got hours and hours to come up with something spectacular."

Unfortunately, it would have to wait, because what he had in mind would not work in their current environment, given that people might start arriving at any time. And that he'd stupidly left all the condoms back at the hotel. But honestly, he'd never have considered a baseball stadium ripe ground for a sexual encounter.

He would not make that mistake twice.

Once he had all his clothes in order, Trinity stood with him at the glass and listened intently as he explained the mechanics of the game—at her request. She asked intelligent questions and genuinely sought to understand the rules, of which there were a lot.

"No wonder you're such a fan of rules." She rolled her eyes good-naturedly. "My eyes glazed over ten minutes ago."

No, they hadn't. She'd absorbed every word, even when he'd gotten entirely too impassioned in his defense of the concept of a designated hitter, which he should hate as a pitcher. Former pitcher.

But all at once, he didn't feel like he had to make the distinction. He was still a pitcher even though he didn't do it professionally any longer. He didn't have to pretend it wasn't a part of him. Trinity hadn't labeled him as a former pitcher or asked if he used to pitch. She'd just understood that baseball wasn't a job, it was his essence.

And then gave him the most amazing sexual experience he could imagine.

How in the hell was he supposed to go back to a one-color, lackluster, *boring* woman after that?

Short answer—he had to. Trinity was temporary. He couldn't be constantly distracted from his life by a sex-on-a-stick marketing executive. Especially not one who'd just demonstrated a remarkable ability to entice him down a rabbit hole of fantasy, which was apparently an Achilles' heel he'd just discovered. They should start talking about exit strategies, stage a public fight. Surely their fake affair had done all the good it was going to do.

But the universe wasn't finished knocking his plans around.

The Mustangs won. And Trinity instantly became a good-luck charm. What was he going to do now, drag her to every game from now until the end of the season?

It was not cool how great that suddenly sounded.

Logan had not been kidding about the interminable rounds of interviews that happened after the game. Trinity lost count of the number of times she heard him repeat the same phrases to yet another reporter.

"Johnson can absolutely repeat that three ninety tomorrow," Logan said easily, which was always followed by, "O'Hare is still on the DL, but we're calling up a reliever from Round Rock who will knock your socks off."

Three ninety—that might have been a reference to the mysterious stat called a batting average that Logan had mentioned earlier. But she wouldn't put money on it at this point. DL meant nothing to her.

It was like a secret code that only the kids in the know could crack, and by the time dinner rolled around, she was jonesing for a glass of wine. Spending an hour on her stuffed-to-the-gills email inbox wouldn't be out of line, either. Her face hurt from smiling as she stood by Logan's side, but his arm never left her waist, and the photos would be brilliant, especially since she'd worn this green dress that would pop on camera.

Several of the reporters asked about her, and Logan eagerly introduced her without a label, but the adoring look he gave her told the story vividly and none of the eagle-eyed cameramen missed that shot.

"You're a much better actor than I would have given you credit for," she murmured as they held hands and dashed for the limo after Logan had finally deemed them both done. "Even I almost believed we were headed for the altar soon."

She'd meant it as a joke, but it twisted at her heart painfully because it was frighteningly easy to pretend the adoring looks weren't faked.

He laughed and kissed her cheek playfully. "Wasn't an act. I'm very fond of you right now."

"Um...really?" She glanced at him askance.

"Did you not see the scoreboard at the end?" He picked up her hand and kissed her fingers, a habit she could get very used to. "Mustangs put one up in the win column. Thanks to you."

"Me?" Had she blown his brains out earlier? She wasn't bad in the pleasure department, but no one had ever actually lost their mind afterward. "Pretty sure I never picked up a bat the whole game."

"You didn't have to. You're good luck. Obviously."

The stress he put on the word *obviously* was like a verbal eye roll, except she still didn't get it. "What, like I'm your Blarney stone now?"

That piqued his interest, and he swept her with a once-over. "Yep, which means I have to kiss you in order to get my dose of luck."

"Now that has possibilities." She let him pull her into his lap to get started on that, which effectively dropped the subject. Fine by her.

By the time the limo reached the hotel, they were both breathless and she'd nearly hit a high C twice as he fingered her under her dress, dipping his talented fingers into the pool between her legs again and again.

"Have dinner with me," he murmured as they hus-

tled through the lobby, ignoring the coaches and players she vaguely recognized. Some of them called out to
Logan, but his gaze was trained on her. Deliciously so.

"Think there will be more photographers here later?"

She glanced around, but the lobby was bare of the
press. For once. Had they finally gotten tired of the
story? Her spine stiffened and a cold chill crept along
each vertebra. If there wasn't a story, what did that mean
for this fake relationship?

"Trinity." He waited until she glanced at him to continue. "I'm asking you to eat with me. Not because it's
good for my ticket sales or to get people to buy more
mascara. Because you have to eat, and why not do it
with me?"

That was too much like a date. Which was a ridiculous thing to be wary of. They'd been on plenty of dates
already. Seen each other naked and put their mouths
on each other in places that would get them arrested if
they'd done it in public.

All at once, she realized—it *wasn't* like a date. She'd
been conveniently standing there when he'd decided
he was hungry, that was all. He wasn't asking her to
spend time with him because he liked her. What if he
had? Would that make a difference? It didn't matter.
He wasn't supposed to like her. She didn't like *him*.
This wasn't real.

Maybe she'd blown her own brains out earlier. Furious with herself for turning into a waffling, idiotic
crybaby, she shook her head, totally unable to fathom
why she couldn't get rid of the crawly feeling on the
back of her neck.

"I need to catch up on work after spending all day
at a baseball game."

"Okay." He nodded like it was no big deal, and why

wouldn't he? It wasn't a big deal. Convenient dining companion was unavailable. So what?

But then he pulled her into his arms by the elevator and gave her a scorching-hot kiss that curled her toes. His tongue talked to hers in a timeless mating ritual that her body responded to in ways no man had ever evoked. He'd literally just made her come in the limo before they'd arrived, and already she was hot for him again, wishing she'd given him a different answer when he'd asked her to dinner.

That's why it was so much better that she'd said no. She didn't need a man to entertain her, and she'd already gotten a couple of orgasms out of the deal. What more did she want?

They weren't dating. This wasn't real. The more she had to remind herself of that, the farther away from Logan she needed to stay.

When she got back to her room, her face still stinging from his stubble, she sat down at the desk to boot up her laptop. The long list of bolded unread emails flashed onto the screen and she nearly cried. Choosing emails over Logan McLaughlin. She was certifiable.

But the job of the chief marketing officer did not stop simply because the woman with the title spent the day watching a bunch of guys in tight pants whack some balls around. The only reason she'd met Logan was because she'd been doing her job, and she needed to keep focusing on that.

An email from Alex with the title Preliminary Sales Numbers jumped out from the screen. She clicked on it.

And blinked. The first line of Alex's email had fourteen exclamation points. For a numbers girl, that was so out of character. Trinity's eye immediately scrolled to the bottom line of the profit/loss statement.

"Holy crap."

It was three hours later in Washington, where Alex lived, but this was too important to wait until tomorrow. Trinity thumbed up Alex on her phone and hit Call.

"Seriously?" she said when Alex answered. "A seven percent increase in sales this month?"

"Would I lie to you?" Alex's indignation spat over the network. "No. I would not, especially not about something as sacred as my balance sheet. You are a star, my dear. Whatever you're doing, don't stop. You've almost singlehandedly halted this smear campaign in its tracks."

Trinity sank down in her seat and shut her eyes. Figured. This had been personal for so long and she'd put her all into reversing the tide. Did this mean she and Logan had to keep going no matter what?

And how long could she actually keep it up without dissolving into a puddle of feminine confusion? Didn't matter. She couldn't quit now.

She plied Alex with a few platitudes, asked after Phillip and the twins her friend was carrying, avoided the topic of Logan like a champ and hung up, determined to make some headway on the campaign for Formula-47 now that everything in her life was on track.

The design program she pulled up sat there mocking her, and her mind drifted to who else? Logan. The way his hair always fell into his face and he shoved it back—she loved touching his hair, threading it through her fingers. Which of course reminded her of his big, solid body over hers...

Funny how that was the strongest image she had of him. But Logan was a closet romantic, and she sighed a little over how he expressed it. Like the single long-stemmed rose he'd given her on their first date, which she might have pressed into a book simply because no one had ever given her a rose that matched the outfit she'd been wearing the day they'd met.

The rose popped out in her mind. And twirled loose some other images. In a flash, the entire Formula-47 campaign unrolled with a million and five different bursts of inspiration.

Her fingers flew to the keyboard and when she next looked up, two hours had passed and she had a crick in her neck.

Bloom. The product was going to be called Bloom.

What better image to sell people on the idea of a cream that regenerated skin cells? *Fyra's Bloom promises to make your skin do exactly that. You'll bloom; your youthful self will bloom; your skin will bloom.* The concept had so many applications, she still had new ad copy and packaging ideas zipping through her mind despite having just devoted two hours to dumping the contents of her brain onto the screen.

It was so perfect, even she was impressed, and once she had the name, the whole thing exploded into exactly the multimillion-dollar marketing push it needed to be—and she had Logan to thank for it.

Before she could think of the ten million reasons it was a horrible plan, she ordered a bottle of the most expensive champagne on the hotel's room service menu. Then she changed into the most seductive black bra and thong she owned, threw on a little black dress that showcased her legs and went to find the only person she had any interest in celebrating with.

When she knocked on his door, he answered with his shirt unbuttoned and hanging loose over his gorgeous chest, as if he'd shrugged it on. His blank expression melted into one of easy appreciation as he swept her with a look that burned her nerve endings.

"Wasn't expecting you. I like the wardrobe change. As long as we're not going out."

She held up the champagne bottle, choosing to ignore his comment about her wardrobe. "I might be convinced to share this with the owner of today's winning baseball team."

"No more work tonight?" He still hadn't moved from the door, blocking the entrance as if to say he had every intention of determining her intent before he let her in. But the sizzling look in his eyes told her he'd clued in pretty fast to why she was here, and it wasn't to ask him to dinner.

"None. I had a breakthrough on a sticky problem and Alex told me we have a seven percent increase in sales this month. I thought you might be up for a celebration."

He stepped back and held the door wide, allowing her to brush past him, but she didn't get far. Snagging her arm, he took the champagne bottle and set it down on the dresser near the door, then whirled her into his arms for a kiss that rivaled the one by the elevator earlier.

Her body went up in flames. Hungrily, she kissed him back as he stripped away every ounce of doubt about what they were doing here with nothing more than his hot mouth on hers.

She moaned and he backed her up against the door, his hard body pinning hers. The contact sang through her and she didn't even mind that they hadn't gotten to the champagne yet. It would keep. And it had been an excuse to seek him out anyway.

She wanted *him*. Against all reason.

Her fingers found the edges of his shirt, and in a flash, she yanked it off to let it drift to the floor, letting her palms delight in the feel of his back, which never ceased to thrill her to the marrow.

"You're barefoot," he growled. "You're too short now."

She laughed as he circled his erection against her stomach, which was so very far north of where they both wanted it. But she could be flexible. "I don't have to be wearing shoes for this."

He groaned as she spun him and pressed him against the door so she could mouth her way down his beautiful abs. That part was like an extra-special treat, perfect for her tongue. The steel bar dipped in and out of the crevices, exploring, tasting. Dipping below the waistband of his pants. But when she reached for the zipper, he stopped her with his hand to her chin, tipping it up.

"Trinity."

All at once, her feet left the floor as he picked her up and carried her to the bed, throwing her down on it. He rolled onto it next to her and immediately picked up that kiss, but now that they were horizontal, it took on new urgency. Their legs tangled together and his fingers tugged on the zipper of her dress, yanking it down until he could peel the fabric from her shoulders, which he followed with his mouth, kissing down the curve of her back as he revealed her skin inch by inch.

When he got the fabric to her waist, he sucked in a breath as he took in her lacy black shelf bra. "That's the most gorgeous sight I've seen all day."

"Better even than the scoreboard?" she teased.

He glanced up at her from under his lashes. "Sure you wanna go there?"

"I, um… It was just a joke."

"That was no joke." He laid her back against the pillow and kissed the valley between her breasts, hooking the straps of her bra with both thumbs to drag them down her arms. "The Mustangs play one hundred and sixty-two games a year. Every win counts, but it's just another day at the office. You can't dwell on one win. We have another game tomorrow with a blank scoreboard."

Transfixed, she watched as he threaded the straps of her bra through his fingers, winding them up until his hands were bound to her arms.

"You, on the other hand," he continued. "Are exquisite. Every time I see you, there's something new to explore. And I was expecting you to be naked under that dress. Because you were earlier. It was a surprise to find this bra. I like that."

Her throat froze as he bent his head to trace the top swell of one breast with his tongue and then dipped behind the wall of lace to curl the tip around her covered nipple. The visual of him licking her underneath her bra put a shower of sparks at her core.

He was telling her that she was indeed the most gorgeous thing to him and he valued her above his team's winning score. What was she supposed to do with that?

All at once, he yanked on the straps, revealing her breasts to his ravenous gaze, and with his fingers still tangled against her arms, it effectively trapped her. Mercilessly, his hot mouth descended on her, licking her, sucking at her sensitive flesh. Moaning his name, she writhed under the sensuous onslaught.

She was supposed to let herself go, obviously.

The little cries she gasped out increased his urgency. He liked it when she made noise, and she liked the result of it. In a matter of moments, he had her clothes on the floor and her naked body decked out on the bed for his blistering perusal. She squirmed a little as his gaze traveled over her and his arousal bulged in his pants, clearly advertising how much he liked what he saw. But he didn't undress, suit up and plunge in. Instead, he rolled her to her stomach and knelt over her, the whisper of his bare torso skating up her back.

The first exploratory touch of his lips on her spine tightened her whole body. He lifted her hair away and licked at her neck, traveling in lazy, delicious circles as if in no hurry to quench the flames he'd ignited under his lips. He kissed the small of her back and kept going across her buttocks, down one leg until he reached her foot, where he sucked at the arch.

The pressure lit her up as he explored an erogenous zone she hadn't been aware she possessed. Gasping as he added his tongue to the party, she nearly came up off the bed.

Apparently he was going for some kind of record in how many new experiences he could find to give her. She did not have a problem with that.

Fabric rustled, and she turned her head to see him finally shedding his clothes. Since that was her favorite show, she watched with unabashed glee. His body was so beautiful. Powerful, sinewy, solid—she could perfectly imagine him in another age as a model for an Italian sculptor.

"Just getting comfortable," he told her with raised eyebrows, but still he didn't seem to be in a hurry to get to the main course.

No arguments on that front, either.

He knelt back in place and licked his way up her leg, lingering around her knee as if he had all the time in the world and was not in fact driving her insane with the combination of his mouth and whiskers on skin that rarely saw more action than a razor blade in the shower. Under the blitzkrieg of Logan's brand of seduction, however, her core exploded with unfulfilled promise, aching to have that same treatment.

He gave it to her. Slowly, he worked his way north until he hit the crease between her legs, and before she had time to wonder about the logistics involved when she was still facedown, he demonstrated by tonguing her from top to bottom, teasing the flesh of her rear with his fingertips at the same time. White lightning forked through her, and automatically, her hips rolled, seeking more, grinding her nub against the mattress so hard, pinwheels of sharp desire exploded everywhere at once.

His fingers worked magic in tandem with his tongue, and she came so fast she scarcely had time to register it was happening before it ripped her apart inside.

Midquake, Logan covered her with his big, solid body, lifted up her thigh and slid home in one fluid, exquisite shot that had them both groaning. His mouth latched on to her neck as he levered out and pushed back in slowly. It was so amazing that she shut her eyes, sinking into the mattress as he sank into her.

It was a long, slow slide into perfection, and she reveled in it, savored each sharp intake of his breath. The feel of him was like nothing she'd ever experienced, lush and tight. He pushed her closer and closer to the edge, one tiny step at a time, and she'd be fine if this lasted for an eternity.

But his urgency increased, driving hers until she couldn't stand it. Pleas fell from her lips as she met him with backward hip thrusts, desperate for more of him, aching for him to fill her faster, harder, deeper. His fingers slid down between the mattress and her stomach to find her center, doubling her pleasure until she came so hard that she had to bite back the scream he'd ripped from her throat.

His teeth bit into her shoulder as he groaned through his own climax, and his undulations set off another round of ripples in her core until she couldn't feel where she ended and he began.

Collapsing to the mattress, he pulled her tight against him, raining weak little kisses on her shoulder where he'd nipped her, apparently in apology, but she didn't care because her body was in a state of bliss.

But then he stiffened and swore. The string of curses was far more explicit than anything she'd ever heard from him, so she half rolled to check in with him when the gush of wetness against her thigh clued her in on the source of his consternation.

"The condom broke," he said tersely. "Extra strength, my ass."

She bit back a curse of her own. But she managed to choke out, "I'm on the pill. It should be fine."

He didn't look relieved. "I appreciate the pass, but it's not fine. I shouldn't have tried that position. I can't even say I'm sorry, because it can't possibly cover how crappy I feel right now."

"It's not your fault," she insisted. "It was an accident."

Just like the first time she'd gotten pregnant. But she hadn't been on the pill then. In all the years since then, she'd never had so much as a scare. It *would* be fine.

His tentative smile went leagues toward quelling her panic, as did the way he held her like he never intended to let go.

"You're very forgiving," he murmured, his voice gruff with an emotion she wasn't sure she understood. "And don't take this the wrong way, but as accidents go, that was an amazing way to have one."

She nodded against his chest because, yeah. The condom had broken for a reason—the sex had been earth-shattering.

Before she was fully ready to lose his body heat, he

rolled from the bed to dispose of the condom remains, then snagged the bottle of champagne, tore off the foil seal and expertly pried it open. "Shall we drink to how real this relationship just got?"

Her pulse jumped into her throat. "What are you talking about?"

Scouting around near the mini fridge, Logan came up with two flutes and poured the champagne. "If you get pregnant, I'll want to be involved. One hundred percent. Can't get more real than the reality of failed birth control."

She took the flute from his outstretched hand and downed it in one gulp, then held it out for more.

"Nothing has failed." And wouldn't. She could not handle another miscarriage, another guy who was fine with sex but not the responsibility that came with it. Sure, men got in line for orgasms, but midnight feedings? Forget it.

Except that wasn't Logan. He'd just said so.

He glanced at her and tossed back his own champagne. "Would a positive pregnancy test be so bad? I mean, let's play it out. I'd be the baby's father, no matter what. We'd have to be coparents, which is a relationship in and of itself. Why not make it official and just coparent as a couple?"

Her heart ached as the sentiment pinged around inside her, seeking a place to land. She wished all at once that he'd meant he wanted to be with her because he'd developed feelings for her. Because he couldn't stand the thought of being apart. But of course he was just talking about the reality of the consequences, not happily-ever-after tied up with a bow.

Fine. She didn't want that. Or at least she was going to convince herself she didn't. Really soon.

Besides, her confusion didn't matter, because there wasn't going to be a pregnancy. Secretly, she'd always assumed that the horrific nature of her miscarriage had rendered her infertile, but she'd never had it officially checked out.

"I can't possibly tell you how much I appreciate that," she said slowly, keeping the rest of her swirl of thoughts under wraps.

His expression warmed. "I've always dreamed of having a family."

"But we don't have any idea if that's what's going to happen," she countered firmly. "Nor will we for some time. Can't we just put it away for now?"

"Sure." He dinged his newly full champagne glass to hers. "For now."

With all of this academic talk about babies and families and a future with Logan in it, a yearning she'd never allowed to gain traction reared its head, settling into a place in her heart. She was pretty sure it wasn't going away any time soon.

Regardless, she was not the right woman to fulfill his dreams, which meant she *should* find a way to stay far away from Logan McLaughlin.

Except she didn't want to.

Eight

Trinity left to go back to her room, but Logan couldn't sleep. The whole day had been wild, and the conversation they'd just had put the crazy sauce on the sundae.

He couldn't stop thinking about the definition of real and how easily he could envision trying to create something that sounded a lot like that with Trinity.

This whole situation had unraveled alarmingly fast.

He'd always thought he'd get married first, then he and his wife would eagerly get on with baby making. They'd take their first pregnancy test together and she'd throw herself into his arms when it turned positive. Happiness would ensue.

Obviously the broken condom had presented another possibility that he might have to get used to—being with Trinity long-term as coparents and maybe more.

Was that what he wanted? Was that what *she* wanted? They hadn't really finished the conversation, not to his satisfaction, but he'd been willing to shelve it for the time being, since there was little reason to discuss it at this point.

Except for the fact that he *liked* the idea of having something real more than he should.

His chest hurt as he reminded himself that he and Trinity weren't at all suited for anything that smacked of real, no matter how he defined it. He'd known from the beginning that they weren't right for each other. Nothing had changed.

And yet everything had changed.

By unspoken agreement, they continued the rest of the trip as planned. Trinity came to the games, his guys played baseball and reporters took pictures afterward of the general manager and his girlfriend. Every time Logan felt like pulling her into his arms to lay a kiss on her that would communicate how much he still wanted her, she came willingly, and he liked her in his bed better than he should as well.

The heat between them sizzled for the camera and sizzled behind closed doors. It was like they couldn't quit each other now that the boundaries had evaporated.

The Mustangs won both games. Naturally. Because of Trinity, he was convinced. His team was convinced, too, and treated her like royalty, sending her flowers and chocolate, cards with funny cartoons. The Mustangs' shortstop, the one who was dating the supermodel against Logan's wishes, convinced his girlfriend to call Trinity about doing ad work for Fyra Cosmetics as a token of goodwill.

When Logan asked her about it, Trinity grinned and told him she had a meeting with the model's manager next week. All in all, it felt like a great match, she said. At night, she worked on a campaign for a new product that she chattered about endlessly during her midnight treks to his hotel room. He loved listening to her talk about the things that mattered to her.

On the plane ride home to Dallas, Trinity sat next to him and they held hands like they had on the way to the West Coast. Somehow it was different. As if the broken condom had created an unspoken agreement that they were testing out how things might go if they did slap a "real" label on their relationship.

If anyone had asked him how he'd like the concept of Trinity Forrester as a permanent lover, he'd have said there was no way it would work. But the last few days proved that was a lie.

What was he supposed to do about that? Unless she got pregnant, there was no call to have any sort of discussion about labels.

Maybe he didn't have to do anything. Maybe he could just let it ride, see how things played out. No one had breathed a word about stopping what they were doing.

Before he could think of a reason not to, he reached out and brushed her jaw with a thumb. Intimately. She didn't miss it and raised her brows at him.

"I wanted to touch you," he murmured. "Sue me."

She laughed. "You don't have to apologize for touching me. I like it. So no lawyers needed."

"Then you should know I plan to keep doing it once we're home," he advised her.

"Oh? I'll be curious how that's going to work when we both have jobs."

"Yeah. We'll have to adjust. Give some things up, maybe." When she made a noise in her throat, he did a double take. "What, you can't make our relationship a priority? We're still trying to generate publicity. Right?"

"Lest you forget, I'm an executive running a multi-million-dollar cosmetics company." She spiked her tone with enough irony to get her point across. "I told you I was working on a new product campaign. I have a strict deadline. Some of us don't get to take trips to the Bay Area and stay in fancy hotels for our work. And when we accompany those of you who do, we have to burn the midnight oil to make up for it."

"I want to spend time with you."

That had not been what he'd meant to say. But now that it was out there…he couldn't help but be curious what she'd do with it.

She scowled as the plane flew through a thick bunch of clouds, temporarily throwing the cabin into shadow. "My career is more important than breezing by your bed to pick up a couple of orgasms."

That wasn't all they had between them, and she knew that wasn't what he'd meant. Her refusal to admit things had shifted between them rankled more than he'd like, but he couldn't force her to be honest. He could only be smart enough to outwit her.

And she hadn't pulled her hand from his, a telling point that he had no problem exploiting.

"Your career is definitely more important than orgasms," he agreed smoothly. "But they shouldn't be exclusive of one another. After all, you found a way to seamlessly integrate one with my job. Let me do the same for you."

"I do like the way you think." There was still a note of caution in her voice. "What do you have in mind?"

"You know the guys need you, right? You're their Blarney stone." He pulled her hand to his mouth for what should have been a quick kiss to her fingertips, but he liked the taste of them so much, he kept them there and talked around them. "Come to the home games with me. I'll pick you up. It's on the way."

"That's not putting my career first, Logan. What happens to your luck if I say no?" Her fingertips curled against his lips in a deliberate caress that immediately made him sorry they were on a plane with a hundred other people.

"You can't. They need you." He was pretty sure she heard the unspoken *I need you* in that as well, but he didn't care. "I'll make it worth your while. Look what I've already done for your career. Seven percent increase in sales isn't anything to sneeze at. I'll figure out a way to blend work and orgasms to your satisfaction. Trust me."

"Okay." She snuggled down in the seat. "It's good for us to keep being seen together anyway."

"Absolutely," he agreed and didn't bother to hide his smile. He'd definitely won that round, and if she wanted to pretend like they were still seeing each other for publicity reasons, he could live with that.

Ticket sales were at an all-time high after a three-game winning streak and the extra boost from the publicity surrounding the road trip he'd taken with Trinity. When he got back to his office at the ballpark, he dived headfirst into his job, which he'd sorely neglected lately. Trinity wasn't the only one with deadlines. Some crucial trade agreements had finally landed on his desk—also thanks to the positive publicity his team had recently seen—and he worked through those without pausing to think about her laugh more than about a dozen times. A personal best.

Trinity came to the games and the Mustangs didn't lose. Their winning streak stretched to five games. Then eight. They were on fire, a flame eclipsed only by the one between Logan and Trinity as they burned up the sheets after games. Sometimes she brought her laptop and worked while the team tore the competition to shreds. Sometimes she put it away and cheered alongside him, occasionally coming up with relevant comments about the action on the field, which showed that she was learning baseball whether she'd meant to or not.

With his fake girlfriend by his side, Logan hadn't watched a game from the dugout since the Mustangs played Oakland. It was a huge shift in his managerial style, one that his coaches hadn't failed to comment on. He let them think it was because Trinity had caught him by the neck and wouldn't let go. Secretly, he was convinced it was part of the good luck that she'd brought them. It was simple math. If he went down to the field, they'd lose. So he stuck to his box and sometimes used the seventh-inning stretch to make sure Trinity felt like she was getting her share of orgasms out of the deal.

The subject of the broken condom hadn't come up, and he trusted she'd tell him if there was something to report. Everyone was getting what they wanted.

A call from the commissioner's office burst Logan's bubble. Cal Johnson, his star player, was the subject of a doping investigation and would likely be suspended pending a long string of meetings that Logan had just been cordially invited to attend. The devastation this news would create could not be overstated. He'd go to the meetings and then see what was what.

Without pausing to question the decision, he drove from his office to Trinity's condo, parked and texted her.

I'm outside. Can I come up?

Her response was immediate.

Of course.

When she opened the door, he forgot everything he'd been about to say, even though he'd seen her yesterday.

She looked so good, gorgeous in a pair of jeans and a T-shirt, which signified she'd had no plans to go anywhere this evening. Of course she had on her facial armor, but her eye makeup was more subtle than normal. But even if she had done her Cleopatra thing, it was part of her whole package, one that he could secretly admit he liked on her. She was bold, outrageous, and he couldn't get enough of her.

"What's up?" she asked, and it was obvious from her expectant expression that she'd assumed the reason for his visit had something to do with their publicity campaign.

"I wanted to see you."

Suddenly, he felt foolish showing up unannounced when in reality, he didn't know what was up. He'd done more wicked things with this woman than with any other woman of his acquaintance, but that didn't give him any better ability to understand how to communicate with her. What was he supposed to do, come right out and admit that he'd been dealt a devastating blow and she was the only one he wanted to be with right now? Because that felt way too real for what they were doing here.

Something shifted in her expression. "Then come in."

He must be more transparent than he thought. He'd never just dropped by like this. Their association started and ended with being seen together for publicity purposes, which he was using as an excuse to continue having sex without committing to anything else.

This was crossing a line. An irreversible line.

He came in.

"I brought you something." Before he changed his

mind, he fished the jewelry box from his coat pocket. "To say thank you."

"For what?" She eyed the long flat box like he'd pulled out a tarantula. "There aren't any reporters here to capture this moment for all posterity. Sure you don't want to wait and give that to me later?"

"No," he growled. "I don't want to wait. This is personal and I don't want it on camera. I…"

Have no idea what I'm doing here.

Instead of floundering around like a moron, he snapped the lid open and showed her the eight-carat diamond necklace he'd painstakingly picked out at the jeweler earlier that day. Before he'd gotten the call from the commissioner's office, finding something to commemorate the Mustangs' eight-game winning streak—a club record—had been his top priority.

"What the hell, Logan." Fire flashed from her gaze, which was not the reaction he'd been looking for. "You can't give me something like that. It's gorgeous."

He couldn't help the laugh that bubbled out. "You have a funny way of showing your appreciation."

Cautiously, as if afraid it might bite her, she held out one finger and touched the teardrop stone. "It's pink. Like the flower you gave me."

Yeah, because the instant he'd seen it, he'd thought of her and how it would look against her beautiful skin. "Does that mean you like it?"

"It's too much for a thank-you." But she nodded. "I like it."

"Shut up and let me put it on you then."

She held up her hair and presented her back without further argument, thank God. He drew the fine chain around her neck to clasp it, then took advantage of the absence of hair to kiss her exposed flesh. She didn't move away. One second against her skin became two, and that was the extent of his self-control.

He mouthed his way to her ear and yanked her backward into his embrace so he could thoroughly ravage her. She melted into his arms and he walked her toward her bedroom, a path he knew from the handful of times they'd ended up naked after games.

But this was the first time they weren't high on the public displays of affection they'd indulged in. The first time he had no excuse to be here other than the obvious—he couldn't stay away.

When he hit the edge of the bed, he lifted his mouth from her neck long enough to strip her and himself, then rolled her to the coverlet. He reached for the condoms she kept in her bedside drawer and then pleased them both by sucking at every one of her erogenous zones until she was wet and swollen enough to take him fully. And she did, with a little gasp that thrilled him.

That pink diamond sparkled in the low light from the neon outside her floor-to-ceiling view of downtown Dallas. He'd never given a woman jewelry before, and the sight of the chain around her neck when she had nothing else on her body except him put a glow in his chest that felt a hell of lot like something that shouldn't be there. As he sank into Trinity again and again, building the fire until they were both moaning with it, the significance of what was happening here overwhelmed him.

This relationship was as real as it got. And he liked that.

He refused to take time to sort that out as she bowed up, thrusting her breasts high. This, he understood, and he took one of those rosy nipples between his teeth, rolling it almost savagely as he thrust faster, spiraling his hips the way he knew drove her insane, silently powering her to a climax that would trigger his. Because they knew each other's bodies, how to please, how to gratify. Physically, they were a perfect match, but not in any other way.

So why was he so wrapped up in her?

They exploded together, and he bit his lip to keep the wash of emotions inside, where they belonged. Afterward, he spooned her into his body the way they both liked it, and she curled into his embrace.

"What's the real reason you came over tonight?" she murmured.

His eyes shuttered automatically. Would she ever *not* be so good at reading him? He couldn't do that with her. It wasn't fair. But that didn't give him any better ability to lie to her, either.

"Johnson is probably going to be suspended. I'm…" What was he? Disappointed? Frustrated? Furious? "Not sure what's going to happen to the team as a result."

"That's crappy." She squeezed his arm with her soft hand. "What did he do?"

"Performance-enhancing drugs, or so they say. They're against the rules. I'm cooperating with the investigation, but I have to go to New York for some meetings."

With neither of them at the away games, the Mustangs' winning streak would most likely come to an end. A brutal but inescapable truth.

"Do you want me to come with you?" she asked, and the note of genuine concern in her voice unfolded all the emotion inside that he'd been trying to keep under wraps.

Silently, he kissed her shoulder, worried something inappropriate—like *yes*—would slip out if he tried to speak. The fact that she'd offered meant more to him than he could say.

Because she deserved an answer, he finally choked out, "No need."

She rolled in his arms and glanced at him, her eyes warm and huge. "This is really bothering you, isn't it?"

He shook his head. Why he'd denied it, when it was obvious she'd already figured that out, was a mystery to him. "I don't know. Yeah. Maybe. I feel like I should have known or something."

Of course doping went on. It was no different today than when he'd been pitching. Everyone knew who was doing it and who wasn't. Logan had never touched the stuff. Fortunately, he'd been good enough that he'd never been pressured like some of the guys.

Maybe Johnson had felt some of that pressure. Had Logan inadvertently been one of those pressure points?

"You didn't do this, darling. It's not on you."

"I'm the boss," he said simply. "And I feel like I failed at keeping my team strong. My dad ran a billion-dollar company for years and years, and he never let anything like this happen to him."

"You're not your dad, Logan. And this is a totally different industry with different rules and strategies. You have to lead like you." She fanned her fingers across his cheek, lightly caressing as she spoke the gospel according to Trinity. "You can't compare yourself to someone who's gone, either. You don't know what might have happened if he'd lived. Maybe someone in his organization would have been brought up on insider trading. Would that have been his fault for hiring someone who made bad choices?"

No. Of course not.

"You're not allowed to make me feel better with logic," he grumbled.

But her point was not lost on him, and some of the

weight lifted. Exactly what he'd hoped would happen when he'd gotten into his car to come over here. Somehow, she made life…brighter.

She laughed and kissed him sweetly. "What if I make you feel better a whole other way?"

Her legs tangled with his, and her wandering hands left no doubt how she intended to make good on that. Since he was pretty sure she could deliver, he let her.

But the whole time he was pondering some huge questions of his own—like, if he wasn't his dad and it was okay to do things his own way, did that mean he could admit he didn't want a nice, unassuming woman? And that maybe the reason he'd never met the right woman had to do with the fact that he hadn't met Trinity yet?

But the most important question of all was, what would she say if he told her that despite all of his objections to the contrary, he was falling for her?

Logan left to go to New York, and Trinity spent a lot of time pretending she didn't miss him.

Funny how she'd never watched sports in her life, would have claimed under oath she hated the concept of grown men throwing balls around in some macho contest. But for God knew what reason, she couldn't go to sleep at night unless a baseball game was on in the background.

The Mustangs' winning streak ended as Logan had predicted that night before he'd gone to the meetings. But they won the next one even though she wasn't at the game to provide good luck, which was such a silly concept. Of course she'd never say that to Logan's face, since he took his superstition so seriously.

He texted her occasionally with updates, but there

was nothing in the messages that indicated his state of mind or whether he was thinking about her like she thought about him. Days stretched into a week, but neither of them approached the subject about when he was coming home or if they'd pick up where they left off when he did.

The Formula-47 marketing presentation had been rescheduled a couple of times due to everyone's crazy travel schedules, but finally, Cass threw a dart at a day and told everyone they better attend or else.

That morning, Trinity had a nearly impossible time dragging herself out of bed. Despite having subscribed to her cable channel's baseball package—which she would deny if anyone called her on it—there hadn't been one game on the night before, and sleep had come fitfully.

While she was busy not sleeping, her mind kept turning over whether Logan was using this trip to New York as a break—from her. Fyra's numbers were up. Logan's ticket sales had gone through the roof. There was little reason to continue seeing each other. But she didn't want to be done. Selfishly, she'd used their publicity campaign to pretend their relationship was real, and she'd liked it far more than she'd expected, especially given that it had been a very long time since she'd spent time with a man outside of bed.

As she dressed in a teal-green suit and did her makeup, she tried on the idea of casually mentioning to Logan that maybe they could still see each other occasionally, if their schedules permitted. Which sounded crappy in her head and probably wouldn't be improved by saying out loud. The problem was that she didn't know how to tell him that she wanted something more, something real, when she had no clue how to do either one.

When she got to the boardroom, Cass was already there, keying in the virtual meeting details on her laptop. Alex and Harper popped up on the split screen TV.

Harper blinked. "Holy crap. What is that around your neck, Trin?"

Fingering the pink diamond that she couldn't bear to take off, Trinity frowned and opened her mouth to say it was a loaner, and to her absolute mortification, she burst into tears instead.

Cass shoved her chair back and rounded the table to pull Trinity into an embrace, a trick and a half since her expanding belly got in the way. But Cass pulled it off with her typical togetherness, murmuring soothing words until the waterworks subsided somewhat.

"I'm sorry," Trinity sputtered. "I don't know what that was about."

Alex and Harper made noises and talked at the same time until Cass shushed them.

"I think I speak for everyone," Cass said with a smirk, "when I say we've all been there. Let me guess. Things with Logan aren't so fake after all."

"That obvious?" Trinity thought about putting her head down on the boardroom table, right on top of the printed materials she'd brought for the campaign. "I don't know what's real and what's fake and why I'm upset about it or what to do about it. I can't sleep and I'm exhausted all the time."

Cass cocked her head. "Have you talked to him about what you're feeling?"

"I can't," she wailed. "He's in New York at meetings about a very big problem for his team and I just want him to come home and sleep with me, like really sleep. I want to wake up with him in the morning and have coffee and just be together. We've never done that. I don't do that with anyone. I don't know why I want that now. It's ridiculous to feel so clingy and out of sorts and—"

"Trinity." Alex's voice rang out from the TV. "Breathe. That sounds like hormones talking. Maybe after your cycle, you'll feel better."

"I'm not on my period," Trinity snapped. Like Alex knew anything about that. She'd only been pregnant for forever. "I'm not even due to start until—"

The first. What was today? Trinity glanced at her phone. The sixth. *Oh, my God.* It was the *sixth.* And she was always so regular.

Panic slammed through her chest as she did the math. It had been almost three weeks since the broken condom incident. With all the baseball games and juggling the Bloom campaign and missing Logan, she'd totally lost track of the calendar.

"I'm sensing we're having a revelation in the works," Harper said cheerfully. "Should we reconvene another day while you go take a pregnancy test?"

A pregnancy test.

The phrase made literally no sense, as if Harper had spoken Swahili. Trinity hadn't taken a pregnancy test in eight years. Because she'd never had the slightest doubt about what the result would be.

"I have a couple of extras in my desk," Cass offered. "From when Gage and I were trying. If you want to know now."

Numbly, Trinity nodded at the woman who had been her best friend since eleventh grade. The distance that had grown between them due to their very different life circumstances vanished. There was no one else she'd want holding her hand as she verified whether her problems with Logan were exponentially greater than she'd supposed.

After an eternity that was really more like ten minutes later, she had her answer.

Amazing how she could actually see the plus sign though all the blurry tears. *Pregnant.* With Logan McLaughlin's baby.

"Should I say congratulations or I'm sorry?" Cass asked quietly.

Trinity didn't answer, just tossed the positive test onto the counter and sank to the ground to put her head on her bent knees. Her whole body shook with a cocktail of nerves and wonder and disbelief and hope. But she had to squash that. Now.

There was no way she'd carry to term. Her body didn't work like that. The little miracle inside would be snatched from her before it had a chance to form, and she'd have to deal with it. Again.

Oh, God. A new round of horror tore through her. What was she going to tell Logan? She'd promised she'd let him know if this happened, but that had been back when she'd been ridiculously certain her birth control would stick. Obviously her pills had failed her and her secret belief that she couldn't get pregnant again was false.

"I don't understand how this happened," she sniffled out brokenly to Cass through the sobs still racking her chest. "What am I going to do?"

"Do you want the baby?" Cass asked, cutting to the chase in her usual style. And of course that was the most important question, and Trinity knew the answer instantly.

"Of course. But that's not in the cards—"

"Stop. You don't know that. You're going to get the best prenatal care possible," Cass countered. "And then we're going to stage sticky-baby sit-ins, ply you with peanut butter, whatever it takes to make this work for you this time. Your womb has had eight years to develop, to mature."

The words filtered through the crushing pain in Trinity's chest but did nothing to absolve it. She couldn't do this, couldn't bear the idea of eventually—soon—having absolute confirmation that she was indeed as broken as she'd always assumed.

But what if Cass was right? What if the baby actually stuck? What if this was the start of the most amazing chapter in her life? For today, right now, she was pregnant with Logan's baby.

Fledgling emotions that she'd never allowed herself to embrace welled up and over with the realization that she had a piece of him inside her, that the universe had conspired to make their relationship real in the most wonderful way possible.

She could admit that when he talked about having a family, she wanted that, too.

And then she realized. She couldn't tell him.

Instead of fearing that he'd take off, the opposite would be true. He'd want to be there every step, to go to the doctor's appointments, pick out a crib. That's who he was, and he'd be devastated if—when—she miscarried. And then she'd have to deal with it alone, because what else would bind them together? He'd be done with her at that point, forever.

She could not take the double loss.

They had nothing between them except a successful publicity campaign and a mass of cells that would never become anything but another heartbreak.

Nine

New York had been brutal. Johnson's forty-five-game suspension destroyed the Mustangs' morale, precisely as Logan had expected when he'd received the verdict.

He'd appealed, naturally, which meant extending his stay longer than he would have liked, but the appeal would take a while to work itself out. Plus, it was strictly a formality; the inquest had Johnson dead to rights, including video of him frequenting the clinic that sold the PEDs.

The whole thing was disheartening.

Once a day, he'd reached for the phone to call Trinity and beg her to fly to New York, just so he could see her. So he could touch her. Hear her laugh, lose himself in her sweet body at the end of a long day of meetings that ripped his team apart. He wanted to be with her, to let her make the horrible reality better.

He wanted more.

But he never dialed. It wasn't fair to start that discussion over the phone. So he held off until he got back to Dallas. While waiting for his luggage to appear from the bowels of the airport, he texted her.

At the airport. Can I come by Fyra to see you?

God, that was bold. Trinity had a job. *He* had a job. Jumping off a plane and driving straight to her wasn't smart. But it was the only thing he wanted to do.

She didn't text him back right away. Probably in a meeting. He went home, which was what he should have done anyway. The house smelled stale and musty from disuse, even though he'd only been gone for a few weeks. The emptiness crawled onto his last nerve, and he hated it. Why had he bought such a monstrosity of a house when he had no one to share it with?

What was today? Thursday? Maybe he'd see if Trinity would ditch work tomorrow and spend a three-day weekend at his place. He'd never brought a woman home, and he could picture Trinity draped across his bed with frightening ease. She'd like his giant marble garden tub, too, he had a feeling. Or rather, she'd like what he did to her while she was in it, which was practically the same thing.

They could order takeout, or maybe he'd cook steaks on the massive grill in the outdoor kitchen that overlooked the pool. Afterward, he'd strip her down to her bare skin, pick her up and lower her into the hot tub at the north end of the pool, cleverly tied into the design via an outcropping of natural river rock.

He checked his phone, but she hadn't texted him back yet. His plane had landed four hours ago. Maybe she hadn't seen the message. He called her this time.

No answer. Fine. She was busy. He'd been gone for a while, and they hadn't really talked much since he'd left Dallas.

Thursday stretched into Friday, and he made the long trek from Prosper to his office in Arlington. The team was in Pittsburgh playing a three-game series and getting their asses handed to them. Myra had some very depressing numbers regarding the decline in ticket sales, which of course had taken a hit with the double whammy of losing the Mustangs' marquee slugger and the lack of new, steamier pictures from the club's favorite poster boy.

But oddly, the most unsettling thing in Logan's world right now was the distinct absence of Trinity Forrester. He missed her keenly, had for weeks, and he could not seem to focus on anything but the three, maybe four, unanswered text messages he'd sent since landing yesterday.

He'd made a mistake not calling her while he'd been in New York, that much was clear. He had to fix it. But if she wasn't responding to his messages or the voice mail he'd left, it was entirely possible she'd lost her phone. It happened.

By Friday night, he couldn't stand it any longer and drove to her condo. Stupid. He couldn't get into the building unless she buzzed him in, but she didn't respond. He could see her Porsche in her designated spot in the parking garage from here.

His temper flared. She was here but not interested in seeing him? That was not cool.

The gods of security smiled on him when a well-dressed couple came out of the building and glanced at the flowers in his hand as he skulked about outside.

"Is she not answering? You must be early, then," the

elderly woman surmised with a misty smile, apparently drawing her own conclusions about the situation. "That's so nice to see."

"Yes, ma'am," he replied, because there was really no other answer.

"Come on, then." She winked and held the door open. Once he was inside…he had no idea if Trinity would even answer the door.

One way to find out. He took the elevator to the fifteenth floor and banged on the door in case she had music on. She answered almost immediately, clearly frazzled, her hair mussed and her ratty sweatshirt a marked contrast to her normal style.

And she wasn't wearing any makeup. She'd literally never been more beautiful. He could not tear his gaze from her.

All the color drained from her bare face. "Logan."

Not expecting him, obviously.

"Surprise." He held out the flowers. His pulse hammered in his throat, and he wanted to sweep her into his arms so badly his hands were shaking.

She eyed the bouquet, her expression frozen. Why wasn't she taking the flowers?

"You, um…didn't respond to any of my messages."

Which judging by the ice chips currently jetting from her eyes, she already knew. "I've been busy. You shouldn't have come by."

The long process of dealing with the PED inquest and fatigue and sheer confusion swirled together to step on Logan's temper. "I wanted to see you. Can I at least ask why the reverse isn't true?"

Warily, she shrugged, but not before he noted her expression. She wasn't as unaffected as she'd like him to think. It settled his temper a touch.

"It was a good time to break things off. I really thought you were on the same page with your lack of communication over the last few weeks."

That speared him right through the chest. She had been avoiding him. On purpose.

"My fault," he agreed smoothly, mystified why there was this distance between them. It felt like she was trying to push him out.

"Let me make it up to you," he said with a smile. "And I don't mean in bed. Unless that's what you want."

Her eyelids shuttered, hiding her thoughts from him. But then, he'd never been able to read her, and the frustration of it almost snapped the stems of the blooms in his hand before he realized the pain in his palm came from the thorns digging into his flesh.

"I'll pass, thanks."

Something was very wrong. Fatigue pulled at her eyes, and all at once, he clued in that her death grip on the door frame wasn't designed to keep him out—she was holding herself up. Alarmed, he made his own guess about why she wasn't wearing makeup. *Idiot.* When her face had drained of color, he'd assumed she'd been unhappy to see him, but in reality, she was sick.

"Is it the flu or something more serious?" he asked.

"It's…nothing," she lied when it was so clearly something. And then she weaved as her knees buckled.

Tossing the flowers, he scooped her up in his arms and shut the door with his foot, refusing to recall the last time he'd done this—when they'd ended up naked together. He couldn't even enjoy the fact that he was touching her again after an eternity apart.

She felt so insubstantial in his arms, weakly protesting as he strode to her bedroom and laid her out on the bed, then wedged in next to her to stroke her hair.

"What is it? Can I get you something? Water or—"

"No, I'm fine," she whispered but her eyes closed and her head pushed into his palm like a cat seeking affection. He was more than happy to give it to her. It pleased him to have his hands on her, even in this small way.

The longer he stroked, the more she relaxed and the less his chest hurt. If she was sick, it explained why she hadn't immediately jumped on his text messages. Probably she'd had one of those silly moments where she'd railed against having him come over and see her without makeup, like he cared about that.

Didn't she know she was beautiful to him regardless?

All at once, she moaned, and it wasn't the good kind. Helplessly, he watched as she turned over, curling in on herself. That was not going to work. But what should he do?

Leaving her on the bed, eyes still squeezed tight, he ventured into her bathroom to see if she had some kind of prescription or over-the-counter medication. And maybe if he found something, it could clue him in to what the hell was wrong with her.

There was nothing on the counter except a small mirrored tray covered with tiny, expensive-looking bottles of perfume. The drawers on the right side of the espresso wood–and–marble vanity held her cosmetics in an array of holders and shelves and various hidey-holes that made his skin crawl, so he shut them and pulled open the cabinet on the left.

Hair spray and various other female things lined the bottom. Including a small white plastic wand with a blue tip. It was face up and he could easily read the words Pregnant and Not Pregnant, next to a plus sign and a negative sign. The big circle prominently featured a blue plus sign.

Logan's brain went fuzzy as his knees gave out and he plopped onto the bathroom floor, half on the short-pile bath mat, half on the white marble tile.

Trinity was *pregnant*. That's what was wrong with her.

"I didn't want you to find out this way." Her low voice floated to him from the doorway.

He glanced up to see her standing there, leaning on the door frame as if it was the only thing keeping her from joining him on the floor.

"What way did you plan for me to find out?" It came out a little harsher than he'd intended, but she'd promised to tell him if this happened, and after ignoring all his messages—

The first tendril of blackness snaked through his stomach as he stared at her flushed face. The lack of welcome. The way she could barely look at him. The cold silence on her end of the line once he'd returned from New York.

"You weren't going to tell me, were you?" How he got that sentence out around the baseball in his throat was nothing short of miraculous.

After the longest pause in history, she shook her head. "But not because I didn't want to. Because—" Something choked off her words and she bent nearly double, scrubbing at her face with the heel of her hand.

He had no trouble filling in that blank. Because it wasn't his baby.

Dark, ugly jealousy flooded his chest as he stared at her. While he'd been falling for her and trying to reconcile all of these strange, wondrous emotions, she'd been seeing other people. Why wouldn't she? They hadn't established any exclusivity. He'd just assumed...

And look where that had gotten him. He followed

the rules and she broke them. She'd never had any interest in having a family, not the way he did. They were always going to be opposites and pregnancy was an irreversible showstopper.

Thank God he hadn't told her he wanted more like he'd half considered while in New York, or this gutting would definitely be worse. Though he had a hard time seeing how when it felt like his stomach was on fire.

How was it possible that he'd been trying to figure out how to take the next step with her while she'd been backing away as fast as she could?

The longer Logan sat on her bathroom floor by the open cabinet, the more Trinity genuinely thought she might throw up right then and there.

Morning sickness had picked a hell of a time to whack her. She'd called in sick to work, a first, but Cass had totally understood despite the fact that she'd never once done it herself.

Trinity was too miserable to care that she was not the champion pregnant woman among Fyra's executives. Now Logan had forced her to deal with him, too.

When she'd opened the door, the first thing that had slammed through her body was relief. *Thank God.* He was here and she didn't have to do this by herself. All she'd wanted to do was fall into his arms, to babble endless words about how much she'd missed him, how beautiful and strong and solid he was. How she knew he was going to make everything better.

Good thing she hadn't. As soon as she realized he was in the bathroom going through her cabinets, she'd hurled herself out of bed to stop him. But it was too late. And judging by the look on his face, this pregnancy conversation was not going to end well.

He was furious.

"You didn't want to tell me?" he ground out through clenched teeth. "You didn't think I had a right to know?"

She'd never heard his voice sound so tightly controlled, so much like he was holding himself in. It frightened her a little. Hadn't he said he wanted kids and had every intention of being in the baby's life? Or had she completely misremembered that?

"I…"

Have no defense.

Really, she didn't. It was only due to her own cowardice that she hadn't told him right away, and as a result, she'd ended up alone over the last couple of days anyway. Nausea turned her stomach over and threatened to expel the chicken noodle soup she'd eaten earlier to settle it.

"I can't do this now," she whispered and sank to the hardwood floor outside her bathroom. She'd thought… well, it didn't matter that she'd thought maybe there was a chance things might magically work out.

"Or ever?" he countered. "You didn't want to tell me because you realized our publicity campaign would be over, right?"

Stricken, she stared at him. He thought she'd kept this quiet because she was worried about *publicity*? "That makes no sense, Logan. Why would our opportunities for publicity end just because I'm pregnant?"

As if that was the most important thing to hash out. He hadn't asked how she was dealing with it, how far along she was. Whether she'd gone to the doctor. None of the things she'd expected. His reaction was almost… cold.

A shiver worked down her spine. This situation was unraveling fast. Potential for miscarriage aside, now that he knew, she'd honestly expected more of a positive reaction.

"Oh, you're right," he said silkily in a dark tone that did not sound like that of a man happy to find out he was going to be father. "Why not continue faking our relationship no matter what? Should be easy. We've been doing it this long, pretending we like each other for the camera. What's an unexpected pregnancy between *friends*?"

There was nothing friendly about his sarcasm, and his point cut through her. He'd been faking it this whole time. While she'd been fighting her feelings and trying not to fall for him, he hadn't been engaged in a similar battle. She'd created a fantasy in her head because he'd given her a few intense looks during sex.

Nothing about their relationship was real. Hadn't she learned that lesson by now? She should have. The pain radiating through her chest was exactly what she deserved for daring to pretend they'd been building something neither of them could walk away from.

"My mistake," she said, proud of how substantial her voice sounded when in reality, her insides felt hollowed out. Fitting that she could fake even this. "I misspoke. It seems as if it might be best if we ended our public relationship. The sooner the better, so we have time to work on a recovery plan."

"And our private one, too." Then he twisted the knife in farther before she had a chance to fully process that. "That's why you didn't tell me, I'm guessing. You knew it would be the end of us and opted to keep the devastation to a minimum."

Miserably, she nodded and shut her eyes against the blackness spreading across Logan's face. At the end of the day, that was the gist of it. She hadn't told him out of pure selfishness. She'd eventually miscarry anyway and there'd be nothing holding them together. But even that had been imaginary, because there was nothing holding them together now, either, apparently.

Why not let him leave now instead of then? It was a simple matter of timing.

Obviously he didn't want her or the baby. Or maybe he didn't want the baby strictly because it was hers. Hadn't he always said she wasn't his type? They were ill suited for each other. That was why he'd always asked her to dress differently, after all.

"I can't do this now, either," he growled. "Congratulations. You've successfully provoked my temper. I have to get out of here."

She scuttled out of the doorway so he could stride from the bathroom. Without a backward glance, he stormed from her condo and took the majority of her heart with him.

The only piece left was tucked in next to the fetus still growing in her womb. For now. She lived in fear of the day she'd wake up in her own blood and know that she was once again alone.

Trinity forced herself to lie in the bed she'd made, continuing to go to work and do her job, but it was far more rote than she would like to admit. Her body hurt all the time and her creativity fled along with her ability to feel anything other than miserable. Thankfully, she'd gotten far enough along in the Bloom campaign that her creative team could run with it.

Logan didn't call. She kept her phone in her hand constantly and cursed every time it buzzed and there wasn't a message from him.

Funny how when he'd been trying to reach her after

returning from New York, each contact point had sliced through her and she'd prayed he'd stop, that he'd leave her alone to figure out how to manage this huge, terrible secret between them.

Now that he had actually broken off all communication, each moment of silence cut even deeper. He really wanted nothing to do with her or the baby. Nor would he be a strong hand to hold when she miscarried. He wasn't the man she'd thought he was, and that was perhaps the worst realization of all.

Late one afternoon, Trinity roused herself out of her stupor to help Harper and Alex throw a baby shower for Cass. It was good for her to stop stewing over things she couldn't change, and it was definitely better to quit dwelling on what had not yet happened, which she had zero control over. Plus, Cass was her best friend, no matter how distant they'd been lately.

Maybe it was time to change that.

Harper flew in from Zurich for the occasion and coupled the trip with some on-site meetings with her lab staff. Alex's twin girls weren't technically due for another six weeks, but her doctor in Washington was convinced she'd deliver any day now, so she participated remotely. As soon as she had her babies, Fyra's CFO would take six months maternity leave.

Once, Trinity would have labeled that ludicrous and pretended a woman's career should trump everything else. When really, it was solely Trinity who had grabbed on to her job with both hands in lieu of seeking what her friends seemed to fall into so easily—a supportive relationship with a husband who loved his wife and couldn't wait to be a father.

Now she could readily admit she was so jealous she couldn't stand it.

As the four pregnant executives gathered in one of the conference rooms at the company they'd built from the ground up, Trinity had enough energy to hug Harper, whom she hadn't seen in person in quite some time. Never would Trinity have thought they'd all have pregnancy in common a few weeks ago. Fyra's chief science officer had finally developed a belly, which she patted when Trinity commented on it.

"Dante calls him Amoeba. I tried to get him to quit, but he thinks it's hilarious." Harper rolled her eyes at her absent husband, whom she'd left behind in Zurich, but only because he was filming his television show about the science of attraction. Otherwise, he'd have been following his wife around like an overprotective caveman, wearing a goofy, adoring expression that communicated how very much he loved Harper and their baby.

Obviously Trinity could use some pointers on how to find a man like that—she should have been watching Dr. Gates's show all along. Then it wouldn't have been such a shock to find out Logan hadn't been falling for her all along like she'd been for him.

Tears pricked at her eyelids and she let them fall. Didn't matter how hard she tried to hold it all in, everything came gushing out anyway. Why fight it?

"Oh, honey." Harper rubbed a sympathetic hand along Trinity's forearm. "It gets better."

Cass settled into the chair on Trinity's other side and drew her into a hug, bopping the balloons tied to nearly every surface of the room. "You still haven't talked to Logan?"

Trinity shook her head against Cass's shoulder without fear, because Harper's combo foundation and powder was bulletproof against smearing. Maybe that could be the genesis of a new ad campaign. But her thoughts refused to jell, like everything else in her life. Her creativity had left the moment Logan walked out of her condo. Which was of course appropriate, because he'd become her muse along with her reason to breathe, the father of her baby and the sole thing that occupied her thoughts 24-7. Ironic, much?

"You have to talk to him," Alex called from the TV screen. "He has legal obligations to you and the baby regardless of whether he likes it or not. Child support, if nothing else. Phillip is texting you the name of a lawyer right now who will get you everything you deserve."

What did she deserve? Half of Logan's fortune? Season tickets to the Mustangs' home games? To be alone because she'd spent her adult life pretending she didn't want the fantasy she'd created with him?

Cass nodded as Trinity sat back in her chair. "Also, things are not always how they seem. I thought Gage and I were destined not to work. And we tried it twice. I never would have predicted that he'd storm into my office with an engagement ring in his pocket."

That was different. Everyone had known that Gage had it bad for Fyra's CEO.

"Phillip kidnapped me on the way home from the hospital, after that time I passed out, so he could talk me out of divorcing him," Alex threw in. "Men can be very unpredictable when they decide they want something."

Harper laughed. "Dante flew from Zurich to Los Angeles, then to Dallas almost back-to-back to tell me he'd screwed up when he left. I've been in love with the man for ten years. I would have taken a phone call. But it was nice to feel like I was his number-one priority."

"You all deserve the happiness you've found," Trinity sniffed. "But you married men who wanted to have children—"

The gales of laughter interrupted her as all three women wiped tears of mirth from their eyes.

"I cannot even begin to tell you how wrong that is," Cass said when she'd gained a small measure of control. "Becoming a father to a one-year-old was probably the hardest thing Gage ever did. He looks like a pro now, but trust me when I say it took a lot of soul-searching on his part to get where he is today."

Harper laced her fingers with Trinity's and smiled. "You do remember that Dante is not the biological father of my baby, right? It took me forever to convince him to go to the doctor with me as my *friend*, let alone for him to decide he wanted to be the baby's father. It nearly broke us apart, but we figured it out. If it's meant to be, you and Logan will, too."

"And if it's not," Alex countered, "you're a strong, independent woman. We'll be there for you as you raise your baby."

"If the pregnancy sticks," Trinity reminded everyone. Because that was the biggest hurdle. It didn't matter what she *wanted*. It mattered what her body decided to do with the baby, which she had no control over. That was probably messing her up the most.

But the love in her friends' words filtered through all the misery anyway, and Trinity smiled for the first time in a long time. "Thanks. You guys mean the world to me, and I appreciate your support. You would have been well within your rights to tell me to stick my self-righteousness where the sun don't shine when I got pregnant."

Harper grinned. "I thought about it. You were pretty smug when you swore you'd never get knocked up. I should get a medal for not blabbing that fifty percent of all pregnancies are unplanned."

"Statistically speaking," Cass said drily, "I think the four of us proved that in spades."

"Yet we still manage to run a multimillion-dollar company." Trinity smiled because that was still amazing. "Even though we apparently suck at launching a secret revolutionary product."

"Hey." Cass scowled. "Your marketing proposal for Bloom is brilliant. We're launching the formula on schedule despite numerous setbacks with first the leak to the industry about our unannounced product, then the legalities of the FDA approval process nightmare. We navigated the tainted samples and triumphed over the public smear campaign. Each of us according to our strengths. That's how we started this business and that's how we'll keep on doing it."

Flinging her red hair over her shoulder, Harper leaned forward with her pit-bull face on. "I wasn't going to mention it since this is supposed to be a party, but since we're on the subject, when I met with my staff earlier, I had an idea for how to catch our culprit. I'm pretty sure I know who it is. But I need everyone's help to close the deal."

"Like a sting operation?" Alex's raised eyebrows reflected in her tone loud and clear. "We're executives, not Charlie's Angels."

"But our lawyer already advised us we couldn't go to the police because we didn't have enough evidence," Trinity argued. Honestly, the whole thing sounded like exactly what she needed to get her mind off everything else. Alex didn't have to ruin all the fun with her logic and reason. "At least hear what Harper has to say."

They bent their heads together and talked through

Harper's thoughts, which Cass insisted was more pro-
ductive and beneficial than opening gifts containing
clothes the baby couldn't even wear until it was born.

Finally, they had a solid plan for how to deal with
the hits their company had taken over the last year as
they dared branch into a new product line. They were
still four strong and would prevail.

Right after they made their plan, Cass, Harper and
Trinity devoured the finger sandwiches and cakes
Melinda, Fyra's receptionist, had ordered for the party.
They were all eating for two, after all.

Ten

Logan groaned and put a pillow over his head as his phone rang at the god-awful hour of…9:45 a.m.

How was it already almost ten? Did he have a game today? Was someone calling to see where he was? His brain would not connect any dots.

Juggling the phone into his hand, he launched out of bed. His big toe collided with the heavy wood nightstand, and when his foot jerked back automatically, his ankle crashed into the bed frame.

The curse he bit out wasn't fit for a dive bar, let alone the caller on the other end of the phone.

"Logan Duncan McLaughlin." His mother's voice had that no-nonsense thing down pat. "I will personally come over there and wash your mouth out with soap if that's how you're going to talk to me."

"Mom, please. I'm really not in the mood."

His head hurt from the copious amounts of alcohol he'd poured down his throat last night after the Mustangs lost their third game in a row. And now he had matching aches on the other end of his body. Rubbing his throbbing toe, he sank back onto the bed and fought the wave of agony inside that was far worse than the physical discomforts.

No amount of alcohol could fix how miserable he was without Trinity.

"Well, I'm sorry, but I don't enjoy learning things about my son's life from the internet." Her tone softened a tad. "I saw an unconfirmed rumor that you and your maybe fiancée broke up. Is it true? Because if it's not over, I still want to meet her."

Wasn't that the million-dollar question? It *should* be over. But he couldn't stop thinking about her, missing her, wanting her.

He flung himself backward to stare at the ceiling in his master bedroom that was far too masculine for his tastes, but the decorator he'd hired had insisted that he'd like the heavy, depressing jewel tones and dark wood. Honestly, he suspected the only thing that would fix it was a woman with a penchant for bold fabrics and colors, who wasn't afraid of slinging her particular brand of style around.

One woman in particular.

He sighed. "The thing with Trinity never really started in the first place. The whole relationship was staged to generate positive publicity for our respective companies."

He braced for censure, shock, something. Who knew what? What he'd just confessed was no doubt blasphemy of the highest order to someone who'd had a great relationship with a man for nearly forty years.

"Oh, please." His mother gave a very unladylike snort. "It might have started out that way, but anyone can take one look at those photographs and see that you care for her."

"Well, *she* doesn't fall in that category, unfortunately." And Trinity was the most important one in that equation. If he wasn't so wrecked, he'd have the energy to get really pissed about it all over again. But all he could muster up was a dose of profound sadness.

"I think you're too close to the situation. She's got it as badly for you as the reverse is true. So why don't you tell me what's really going on?"

He almost smiled at that, but only because his mom sounded like Trinity, reading his mind and his moods with ease. "How do you know anything is going on? We had a fake relationship and now it's over. What more could there be?"

Everything. And nothing. Because he'd been naive enough to think what they'd had was special. Real. Instead, it was all an illusion, and he'd walked right into it without even realizing it was vanishing around him until it was gone.

"Please. I was married to your father, wasn't I? The day I can't understand a man with McLaughlin DNA is the day I gladly go to meet my maker. Spill. Or I'm coming over there."

Which was not an idle threat. She'd do it, too, and drag the whole story out of him while cooking him something full of fat and calories and love.

Suddenly that sounded so nice, his throat went tight. "I'd be okay with that."

"Oh, sweetie. Is it that bad?"

"She's pregnant." Why had he blurted that out? It was too early for this kind of ambush.

"What? Give me that girl's phone number right now!" His mother's outrage nearly burned up Logan's phone, his fingers and his ear. "I cannot believe that woman would try to use you to extort money—"

"Mom, she didn't try to get money out of me."

"She…tried to pass the baby off as yours?" Obviously that was the more delicate issue in her mind.

"No, she didn't do that, either."

"So. Let me get this straight. You had a fake relationship with her but you had an agreement to not see other people?" When he muttered *no*, she blurted, "I'm drawing a blank here, then. It's like you gave up within sight of the finish line. What did she do that was so horrible that you can't tell her how you feel?"

"The baby is not mine!"

"So? What does that matter?"

The phrases echoed through his head, condemning him, because suddenly, he didn't know the answer. It felt like there should be some kind of rule that said you didn't stay with a woman who'd gotten pregnant by another man. But Trinity had never conformed to the rules, and she'd certainly proven her ability to get him to break them often enough as well.

"I—"

"Have a temper and let it ruin your relationship?" she guessed easily. But his mom wasn't done icing that cake. "Do you love her?"

"Of course I do." He blinked. "I mean…I don't know. Yeah. I thought I was moving in that direction, but it all fell apart."

"Honey, you basically just told me that a pregnant woman had a billionaire on the hook and chose to be honest with you about what was going on. Sounds like a keeper to me. Get off your butt and go get what you want."

Was his mother *daring* him to be with Trinity anyway? "It's not that simple."

"Then move on," she advised. "Put this chapter behind you. There's this really nice girl I want to introduce you to. She just joined my church. That's why I called, actually—"

"Thanks, Mom, but no."

He stood up as conviction roared through his chest. He didn't want a nice woman. He wanted a shocking one who didn't put up with his crap and dared him to take what he wanted. A woman like his mom.

Maybe he was more like his father than he'd credited.

For the first time since he'd left Trinity's condo, his world made sense. He was in love with Trinity and he'd screwed up by walking out on her. Period. Everything else was just incidental.

Now he had to convince her that while they were busy faking it, reality had crept up and changed everything.

The sting operation—such as it was—had been a huge success. Fyra's four executives had delivered Harper's lab manager into the hands of the police, along with her venom-filled confession recorded digitally on Trinity's phone.

It was so great to have finally taken control of *something*.

"That woman deserves to burn," Harper spat as the detective the Dallas police department had sent finally left. "Imagine the nerve. Assuming she deserved any credit for Formula-47. That was my baby. I gave up my life for two years to develop it. All she did was take notes. *Dante* did more than she did when he created the new FDA samples after *she* ruined the first ones."

The woman had been so angry about the perceived lack of credit that she'd confessed to causing all of their problems in hopes of ruining Harper for the snub. In reality, the lab manager had little to do with the creation of Bloom. Psychological screening was definitely in order.

"It's over now," Cass said soothingly and glanced at Trinity's phone, which was still on the table in front of her after she'd played the recording for the detective. "We should go celebrate."

Trinity sank into a swivel chair in the conference room where they'd met with the police, clutching her weak stomach. "That doesn't look like the face of a CEO who just plugged the leak in her company."

"I, um…think you should see this." Cass held out Trinity's phone to show her a text message. From Logan. "I didn't mean to read it, but it popped up with the preview."

"It's okay."

Numb, she tapped up the whole message. She probably wouldn't have read it now—or ever—if Cass and Harper hadn't been sitting there staring at her. But she had to talk to him sometime. Avoidance wasn't a good coping mechanism.

The text jumped off the screen.

We need to stage a public breakup. I left a ticket to today's game at will call. Come by before the seventh inning and we'll get it on camera.

It was a good idea. Brilliant, in fact. Maybe they could still generate some publicity with another fight. Except her stomach heaved so much that she genuinely feared she might throw up.

So this was it then. Logan was really lost to her. In

keeping with the painful theme of their relationship, it didn't seem real.

"Want me to drive you?" Cass asked quietly.

Disoriented, Trinity nodded. Cass didn't try to talk to her on the way to the stadium, a blessing because she didn't know what she'd say. At will call, Cass insisted on buying her own ticket, even though Trinity tried to pay for it as a thank-you for driving her. She couldn't have done this alone. For a woman who claimed to value independence, she'd grown remarkably unable to stand on her own two feet lately.

Per the additional instructions Logan had texted her en route, Trinity found the security guard expecting her, and he led both women through a warren of hallways and out onto the field where Logan was supposed to meet her. They hung back, well out of the way of the cameramen and other personnel.

The game was in progress. Top of the seventh, so she'd made it before the stretch as instructed. The Mustangs were up to bat, two men on base and two outs. She eyed the lineup. The next batter couldn't afford a sacrifice fly because the runner on second wasn't fast enough to tag up—God, what was she doing? Where did all that stuff even come from?

Well, no mystery there. Logan had infused her with his passion so easily because she'd loved hearing him talk about baseball.

LA's left-handed pitcher took out the right-handed batter in three easy strikes and the inning was over. The players streamed from the field, and a woman in a US Air Force dress uniform sang "God Bless America." Trinity had seen this routine several times now, but never from the field. The perspective was dizzying.

As the last notes faded, a figure shadowed the stadium lights, and Trinity glanced up.

Logan. Big, beautiful and such a hit to her already strung-out nerves. How dare he stand there with that killer smile, looking so amazing that her knees actually buckled before she could catch herself? Apparently her body hadn't gotten the memo that she didn't go for men who bailed when the going got tough.

"You rang?" she called out sarcastically and crossed her arms before he noticed her hands were shaking. "Looks like even I couldn't save Walker's RBI, so your plan to get your good-luck charm on the field failed. LA's reliever is hot."

He shrugged good-naturedly. "Win some, lose some."

"Close your mouth, Trinity," Cass muttered from behind her. "There's a camera on you. And it's streaming your conversation to the big screen."

Somehow Trinity hinged her jaw back into place, but not because of the camera. The whole point of her being here was to put this madness behind her once and for all, and she had to actually talk in order to get this argument started.

No matter how much it hurt.

"Win some, lose some?" she repeated incredulously. "Who are you and what have you done with Logan McLaughlin?"

Because the guy she'd known would never say that. Maybe that was part of the point. She hadn't ever really known him.

His brow arched. "I told you, the scoreboard is not the most beautiful thing in my world. You are."

Something was off here. They were supposed to be staging a public breakup, not rehashing stupid things they'd said to each other. Hands jammed down on her hips, she scowled. "You hate my clothes."

"I do like you better naked," he agreed readily. "But I don't hate your clothes. I just like the ones I pick out above the ones you pick out. But we can compromise."

"Compromise?" Now she felt like a parrot. "Can you even spell that? You're dictatorial, inflexible and frankly, I have no idea how you walk around under the weight of all the rules you've got slung over your shoulder."

Now they'd get into the knock-down, drag-out part of the agenda. He hated it when she made fun of the stick up his butt.

But instead, he nodded. "That does sound like me. That's why I need a woman like you in my life to shake things up and point out when I'm being too narrow-minded. I lost the best thing that ever happened to me when I walked away. So this is your public apology. I'm sorry."

The stadium lights swirled into a big blob as her vision tunneled and the roar of the crowd's approval swelled up and over the sudden pounding of her pulse. This wasn't an argument. He'd lured her here under false pretenses so he could *apologize*?

"What are you doing?" she whispered. "We're supposed to be breaking up."

"But that's not what I want." Logan inched forward on the grass, capturing her hand in his and bringing it to his lips like he'd done so many times. "Forgive me. I didn't handle our last discussion well and I'm asking you for another chance. Publicly. I'm also giving you the opportunity to humiliate me, because I deserve that far more than I deserve you."

Her throat clogged with unshed tears that shouldn't

be there. None of this could be real. "Why will this time be any different?"

Which was not at all what she should have said.

There was an angle here that she wasn't getting.

That's when he smiled and the tenderness in his expression washed over her. "Because this time, I'm admitting right up front that I'm in love with you."

Blood rushed from her head so fast that she nearly passed out. When she wobbled, Logan's expression shifted instantly to concern and he waved the camera off, scooping her up in his arms.

This time, she wholeheartedly agreed with his tactics, because holy hell. "Did you just tell me that you're in love with me?"

"It's okay," he murmured as he carried her through the warren of halls. They passed people getting ready for the eighth inning now that the team owner's theatrics were over, but no one stopped them and finally he found a private, unlocked room. "I'm not totally used to it yet, either."

He settled her into a chair and knelt by her feet, caressing her face with questing fingers, likely to verify whether she was about to face-plant on the floor. His heat faded from her body far too fast. All she could do was drink in his precious face, hair falling into it and all. God, she'd missed him, missed the feel of him under her fingers, missed the rush of him through her blood.

"Why would you say something like that?" she burst out. Now that they were alone, all her emotional consternation over the last few days squished her chest. Which wasn't going to work. She needed to be calm and rational instead of a hairbreadth from flinging herself back into his arms, where she felt safe and beautiful and loved. "None of what we had was real."

"Because I'm trying to make it crystal clear that what we had before might have been fake, but what I want to have going forward isn't." Quietly, he surveyed her. "We're starting off with no misunderstandings. The way I feel about you *is* real. I should have told you before now."

"But I don't understand." Her voice gained a little strength as some of what he was saying filtered through the ache in her heart. "You didn't want anything to do with me or the baby. What changed?"

He didn't so much as blink. "I realized that I was being shortsighted by letting something like a past relationship stand in our way. I can accept a baby that isn't mine. As long as you come along with it."

The ground slid away at an alarming rate. Words. Buzzing in her ears. No context.

"What past relationship?" And then *isn't mine* registered. "Are you accusing me of having *slept* with someone else while we were dating?"

Before she could stop herself, she slugged him on the arm. Her knuckles glanced away and started smarting like she'd hit a brick wall. Which wasn't far off.

"It's okay," he said soothingly. "We didn't have an exclusive agreement. I was being a Neanderthal about it."

"The baby is yours, idiot," she ground out through clenched teeth as his face went ghost white. "*Men.* Oh, my God. Really? When would I have had time, Logan? Of *all* things. I went to four million baseball games with you. I went to *Oakland*. What do I have to do to prove that I was invested in us? If you've made me miserable for the last few days because you didn't bother to ask me one of the most basic questions—"

Air whooshed from her lungs as he snatched her into

his arms, holding her so tightly she couldn't breathe. But she could still hear him repeating *sorry* over and over.

Squeaking, she shoved at his rock-hard pecs until he eased up a bit. "Seriously? You thought the baby wasn't yours?"

Oh, God. All of this started making a wonderful, terrible sort of sense.

"I...made my own assumptions about why you didn't tell me right away," he confessed miserably. "I'm so sorry. I should have clarified before storming out. It's really mine? I'm going to be a father?"

As she nodded, the clearest sense of wonder stole over his features and his smile spread through her veins, warming her. "Really. No question."

He wanted the baby. Raw, gorgeous emotion beamed from deep inside him so clearly that those unshed tears inside her welled up and over, falling down her cheeks unchecked. This was what it *should* look like when you told a man you were having his child. Beautiful. Bonding. Amazing.

His smile turned a little misty. "You're right. I'm an idiot. And you can feel free to call me one for the rest of your life."

"Are you going to be around that long?" she murmured, her eyes widening as he pulled a square box from his pocket and unhinged the lid. "What are you doing?"

Exactly what she'd dreamed of, obviously. Giving her the one thing he'd never given anyone else, because he thought she deserved the unique experience reserved for the future Mrs. McLaughlin.

"Proposing," he verified as her stomach twisted. "But not on camera. Because this is for me and you only."

The ring sparkled in the light, shooting pink flares into her eyes and nearly blinding her to all the huge problems with what he was about to do. Everything came to a head in one horrific shot. She swallowed and shook her head. "No, you can't."

He eyed her. "Why not?"

I might say yes.

He deserved better than a defective bride. Her frozen hands wouldn't move, wouldn't stanch the flow of pain. "You didn't ask why I kept such a big secret. I have a history of miscarriages. This baby might not ever be born. Then where will we be?"

His eyelids shuttered for a moment, and when he opened them, the compassion there nearly crushed her anew.

"Let's start over." His voice broke as he held out his hand, which she didn't hesitate to take, letting his big palm cover hers. "My name is Logan McLaughlin and I own a baseball team that I bought because I thought it was going to fill a void in my life that throwing out my elbow had created. I was wrong. *You* fill the void. I love you. Whether you can carry a baby to term or not."

Finally, she'd stripped him of his conservative armor and gotten to the real man underneath. Her heart filled so full of him that she could hardly speak. But she had to as she pumped his hand slightly for good measure. "My name is Trinity Forrester and I married my job as a marketing executive because I thought I was too broken to ever have what I really wanted. *You*," she clarified as he raised a brow in question. "I want you. For real. Forever."

And he'd uncovered the woman behind the outrageousness. Probably he'd done that the first day. Because he was exactly her type, a strong, solid man who stuck around no matter what.

Whether she lost this baby or it decided to grace them with its presence after all, Logan would be there by her side, holding her hand. Loving her. He was her every fantasy come to life, and she was holding on tight. Not because she feared he'd vanish. But because she never wanted to let him go.

Epilogue

Four local TV stations, two TMZ correspondents and a liaison from *Entertainment Weekly* covered the wedding of the year between Trinity Forrester and Logan McLaughlin. The mother of the groom told anyone who would listen that she was going to be a grandmother.

Bloom launched the very next day, but Trinity and Logan were busy cheering the Mustangs as they won their seventh straight game. They planned to take a honeymoon somewhere exotic and expensive after the season was over and before Trinity got too big. At twelve weeks, Dr. Dean had proclaimed Trinity's pregnancy mostly out of the woods. There was still a chance she'd miscarry, but the odds went down significantly enough that Trinity stopped walking around on pins and needles.

Her condo in Dallas sold in one day and she moved to Logan's Prosper estate, which she'd fallen in love with the moment she'd laid eyes on it. Slowly, her style permeated the property until it became theirs. They bought two dogs, a male and a female, and named them Nolan and Estée.

Best of all, Logan had an extra closet built off the master bedroom for Trinity's clothes and shoes and almost never complained about what she wore from it—as long as she let him take it off her at the end of the day. Win-win in her book.

The positive publicity from the apology heard round the world, which went viral nearly instantaneously, guaranteed the launch of Bloom would go well, and it did. Its success far exceeded the expectations of Fyra Cosmetics' C suite, and Alex celebrated by giving birth to healthy twin girls. Phillip, the proud father, sent his private plane to Dallas to collect her friends, and Cass and Trinity in turn collected their husbands to travel with them. Harper flew into Washington, DC, from Zurich with Dante, and the six of them gathered at the hospital to meet the babies.

Logan's big hand never let go of Trinity's as they stood at the end of the bed. Her face hurt from smiling. The babies were so precious, and Phillip's and Alex's expressions as they each held one were priceless. *Awestruck* barely covered it.

"That's going to be us soon," Logan murmured in her ear.

"We don't know for sure," she whispered back, because this was Alex's day, not hers, and negative talk had no place here. "I'll be okay either way."

And she would be. Logan had told her several times that if the worst happened, they'd look into adoption. Or wait and try again. Or buy a horse. All of the above. Whatever she wanted. That fit perfectly with her plans, because she wanted it all—a family with a man who loved her by her side.

As she glanced around the hospital room at the three women with whom she'd built a cosmetics empire, their husbands, children, babies to come…it didn't matter what happened with her own pregnancy. She had it all already.

* * * * *

If you loved the LOVE AND LIPSTICK *series,*
where mixing business with pleasure
leads to love for four female executives,
pick up these other sassy, sexy reads
from Kat Cantrell!

MARRIAGE WITH BENEFITS
THE THINGS SHE SAYS
THE BABY DEAL
PREGNANT BY MORNING
MATCHED TO A BILLIONAIRE

***

MILLS & BOON®
Hardback – February 2017

ROMANCE

The Last Di Sione Claims His Prize	Maisey Yates
Bought to Wear the Billionaire's Ring	Cathy Williams
The Desert King's Blackmailed Bride	Lynne Graham
Bride by Royal Decree	Caitlin Crews
The Consequence of His Vengeance	Jennie Lucas
The Sheikh's Secret Son	Maggie Cox
Acquired by Her Greek Boss	Chantelle Shaw
Vows They Can't Escape	Heidi Rice
The Sheikh's Convenient Princess	Liz Fielding
The Unforgettable Spanish Tycoon	Christy McKellen
The Billionaire of Coral Bay	Nikki Logan
Her First-Date Honeymoon	Katrina Cudmore
Their Meant-to-Be Baby	Caroline Anderson
A Mummy for His Baby	Molly Evans
Rafael's One Night Bombshell	Tina Beckett
A Forever Family for the Army Doc	Meredith Webber
The Nurse and the Single Dad	Dianne Drake
The Heir's Unexpected Baby	Jules Bennett
From Enemies to Expecting	Kat Cantrell

MILLS & BOON®
Large Print – February 2017

ROMANCE

The Return of the Di Sione Wife	Caitlin Crews
Baby of His Revenge	Jennie Lucas
The Spaniard's Pregnant Bride	Maisey Yates
A Cinderella for the Greek	Julia James
Married for the Tycoon's Empire	Abby Green
Indebted to Moreno	Kate Walker
A Deal with Alejandro	Maya Blake
A Mistletoe Kiss with the Boss	Susan Meier
A Countess for Christmas	Christy McKellen
Her Festive Baby Bombshell	Jennifer Faye
The Unexpected Holiday Gift	Sophie Pembroke

HISTORICAL

Awakening the Shy Miss	Bronwyn Scott
Governess to the Sheikh	Laura Martin
An Uncommon Duke	Laurie Benson
Mistaken for a Lady	Carol Townend
Kidnapped by the Highland Rogue	Terri Brisbin

MEDICAL

Seduced by the Sheikh Surgeon	Carol Marinelli
Challenging the Doctor Sheikh	Amalie Berlin
The Doctor She Always Dreamed Of	Wendy S. Marcus
The Nurse's Newborn Gift	Wendy S. Marcus
Tempting Nashville's Celebrity Doc	Amy Ruttan
Dr White's Baby Wish	Sue MacKay

0117 GEN STD LP

MILLS & BOON®
Hardback – March 2017

ROMANCE

Secrets of a Billionaire's Mistress	Sharon Kendrick
Claimed for the De Carrillo Twins	Abby Green
The Innocent's Secret Baby	Carol Marinelli
The Temporary Mrs Marchetti	Melanie Milburne
A Debt Paid in the Marriage Bed	Jennifer Hayward
The Sicilian's Defiant Virgin	Susan Stephens
Pursued by the Desert Prince	Dani Collins
The Forgotten Gallo Bride	Natalie Anderson
Return of Her Italian Duke	Rebecca Winters
The Millionaire's Royal Rescue	Jennifer Faye
Proposal for the Wedding Planner	Sophie Pembroke
A Bride for the Brooding Boss	Bella Bucannon
Their Secret Royal Baby	Carol Marinelli
Her Hot Highland Doc	Annie O'Neil
His Pregnant Royal Bride	Amy Ruttan
Baby Surprise for the Doctor Prince	Robin Gianna
Resisting Her Army Doc Rival	Susan MacKay
A Month to Marry the Midwife	Fiona McArthur
Billionaire's Baby Promise	Sarah M. Anderson
Seduce Me, Cowboy	Maisey Yates

MILLS & BOON®
Large Print – March 2017

ROMANCE

Di Sione's Virgin Mistress	Sharon Kendrick
Snowbound with His Innocent Temptation	Cathy Williams
The Italian's Christmas Child	Lynne Graham
A Diamond for Del Rio's Housekeeper	Susan Stephens
Claiming His Christmas Consequence	Michelle Smart
One Night with Gael	Maya Blake
Married for the Italian's Heir	Rachael Thomas
Christmas Baby for the Princess	Barbara Wallace
Greek Tycoon's Mistletoe Proposal	Kandy Shepherd
The Billionaire's Prize	Rebecca Winters
The Earl's Snow-Kissed Proposal	Nina Milne

HISTORICAL

The Runaway Governess	Liz Tyner
The Winterley Scandal	Elizabeth Beacon
The Queen's Christmas Summons	Amanda McCabe
The Discerning Gentleman's Guide	Virginia Heath

MEDICAL

A Daddy for Her Daughter	Tina Beckett
Reunited with His Runaway Bride	Robin Gianna
Rescued by Dr Rafe	Annie Claydon
Saved by the Single Dad	Annie Claydon
Sizzling Nights with Dr Off-Limits	Janice Lynn
Seven Nights with Her Ex	Louisa Heaton